M

A JEWELER'S EYE FOR FLAW

A Jeweler's Eye for Flaw

STORIES

CHRISTIE HODGEN

University of Massachusetts Press   Amherst and Boston

This is a work of fiction, and any resemblance
to persons living or dead is coincidental.

This book is the winner of the Associated Writing Programs 2001 Award
in Short Fiction. AWP is a national, nonprofit organization dedicated
to serving American letters, writers, and programs of writing.
AWP's headquarters are at George Mason University, Fairfax, Virginia.

LC 2002007577
ISBN 1-55849-374-3

Designed by Kristina Kachele
Set in Heliotype and Monotype Walbaum by Graphic Composition, Inc.
Printed and bound by Maple-Vail Book Manufacturing Group

Library of Congress Cataloging-in-Publication Data

Hodgen, Christie, 1974–
  A jeweler's eye for flaw : stories / Christie Hodgen.
     p.   cm.
"Winner of the Associated Writing Programs 2001 Award in Short Fiction."
     ISBN 1-55849-374-3 (alk. paper)
     I. Title.
  PS3608.O47 J49 2002
  813'.6—dc21

2002007577

British Library Cataloguing in Publication data are available.

FOR BART

ACKNOWLEDGMENTS

These stories originally appeared in the following journals and anthologies:

"Going Out of Business Forever" in *Notre Dame Review*, no. 8 (Summer 1999), and *Quarterly West*, no. 53 (Fall 2001)

"The Hero of Loneliness" in *Meridian*, no. 6 (Fall 2000), and *New Stories from the South 2001*

"A Jeweler's Eye for Flaw" in *Georgia Review* 56, no. 1 (Summer 2002)

"Sir Karl LaFong or Current Resident" in *Bellingham Review*, no. 48 (Spring 2001)

"Take Them In, Please" in *Greensboro Review*, no. 69 (Spring 2001)

"Three Parting Shots and a Forecast" in *Scribner's Best of the Fiction Workshops 1999*

I wish to extend my gratitude to the following people:

Bart Patenaude, my Rushmore.
My dear friend Christine Sneed, the girls from 424 and the crew
at store 3, my teachers—J. C. Levenson, George Garrett, John
Hildebidle, Tony Ardizzone, and Margaret Smith—my agent, Kit
Ward, and my family, especially John, Doreen, Mae, Janice, and Joe
Hodgen, Roomie and Bob St. Onge, and Eldora Reed.

I would also like to thank the people at the following organizations:
the Associated Writing Programs, the University of Massachusetts
Press, the Kentucky Foundation for Women, the Kentucky Arts
Council, and all of the literary journals who gave me a running start.

CONTENTS

A JEWELER'S EYE FOR FLAW

A Jeweler's Eye for Flaw

The times are strange, and the ways we kill ourselves even stranger. In the course of a year we receive letters from our missing fathers— men who have worked their whole lives as lumberjacks, grave- diggers, butchers, fishermen, ambulance drivers, marines, and gar- bage men—but now these fathers send word they're recovering from strokes in government-funded rehab centers, and it's nothing but oatmeal dribbling down the chin, elastic bands cinched around the upper arm, serums shot into blown veins, the glorious state of bed sores and perpetual pajamas. They write this with their left hands, their script wild and slanting across the page, like lost kites. In the course of a year there are whole factories of workers laid off from their jobs. Our families change. Broke and hopeless, our moth- ers give up on the tired and maddening routine of child care, all the scolding and straightening, and they seek refuge in dummies. They become ventriloquists, and start speaking to us through our child- hood teddy bears, which they wave amicably in front of our faces, making the bears talk to us in high, girlish voices, even allowing the bears to turn cruel, to say what our mothers themselves have always thought but never voiced, that we'll never amount to anything but homeless whores. In the course of a year a boy at our high school attempts three suicides, lighting himself on fire, slitting his wrists, and swallowing pills. All year he wears the scars of his efforts with a spooky stateliness, and we watch his every move. We spread rumors, saying that he keeps a rope coiled like a poisonous snake in his hip pocket, that he plans to strangle the first person who speaks to him. We are trapped in high school's interminable final year. We are still young enough to believe that these troubles are temporary, to believe the promises of politicians in this election year as they talk into television cameras about economic recovery and personal responsibility, and we think we see, in the slender gleam of their tie clips, an end to this suffering, this staleness, this strife. All of this happens over and over again, in slightly different forms, in every suburb of every failing industrial city. We are, as everyone is happy to remind us, nothing special.

Ever since my father took the car and started north, looking for work, my mother and I walk a mile every Wednesday to the grocery store. We fight in the florescent-lit aisles, comparing the merits of each brand of chocolate-covered marshmallow cookie, of frosted cereal and canned ravioli, of bargain diet soda and frozen pizza.

"I must have my Pecan Sandies," my mother says, waltzing with the shopping cart. Her long, gray hair streams behind her like a cape. She is the superhero of shortbread, swooping down to rescue five bags of homeless cookies. A former music teacher, she is the kind of person who makes theatrics out of the most ordinary desires. She holds up a bag of cookies like Scarlet O'Hara with the raw carrot in the famine scene from *Gone with the Wind*. "God as my witness," she says, "I'll never go hungry again!" She tosses the cookies in the cart. "Pecan Sandies," she whispers, "I'm going to eat you alive."

We pause, as we do every week, to survey the many brands of hair color that my mother is considering buying. She has debated for months the benefits and drawbacks of hair dye. "I don't want to look like a hooker," she says this week. "You remember what your grand-mother looked like, right?" I am unmoved—a sulker and a moper, an eye-roller. Although I can't help but smile when, on the walk home, my mother points out a conspicuous van stopped at a red light. JOE'S BOLT AND SCREW is painted in red letters across the side of the van. "Funny," my mother says. "Usually joes screw and bolt."

This is, my mother reminds me, the trail of tears: Take only what you can carry. We walk home with our awkward bundles, stopping every hundred yards to shift our grip on the grocery bags. It is fall. The sky is dark by six and the grass is stiffened with frost. The trees are bare, their lost leaves blowing from lawn to lawn. This is the sea-son that always gives the impression that time has stopped. I fear that the semester will go on forever, that I will chant for all eternity conjugated verbs in Spanish class, that I will spend the rest of my life stuck somewhere in the depths of *Middlemarch*, that I will de-liberate infinitely which colleges to attend without ever completing an application, that I will evermore play my clarinet in the second row of my high school concert band, knowing without question that nothing I do or fail to do will be noticed or even heard.

"Stop sulking," my mother says. "Other kids your age have fun. They enjoy life. They live a little."

My mother refers to a group of teenagers who have just run past us, whooping and laughing and carrying large pumpkins. "We rock!" one of them yells. "We fucking rock!" They howl. There are five of them, dressed identically in black unitards. I don't notice un-til one of them turns around that the fronts of the suits are painted with glow-in-the-dark bones, that these five kids my age are having fun, enjoying life, living a little, while dressed as skeletons.

"We forgot the fucking candy," my mother says, and sighs. It is Halloween, a detail escaping both of us until now.

"I completely forgot," I say.

"Me, too." She looks dejectedly into her sack of groceries.

"You can give out Pecan Sandies," I say.

My mother straightens to her full height, appalled. "Watch your mouth," she says. Just then I hear footsteps. Someone is running toward us. And when I turn to look back something brushes my shoulder, someone's chilly white bedsheet, someone's Halloween cliché, someone's lousy costume. It clings ever so briefly to my shoulder, then whisks away, the tail of a speeding ghost in black combat boots.

"I think that was James Woodfin," I say to my mother. "I think those were his boots."

"How's he been doing?"

"Okay," I tell her. "He's got scars on his neck and all up one side of his face."

"Poor thing," says my mother. Her mouth is full. She has already broken into one brilliant yellow bag of Pecan Sandies. "Never forget," she tells me, "I named you after the thing I love most in the world.

"I know," I say. My name is the worst name in the world, stomach-turning, sickly sweet.

"Watch out, Sandy," says my mother, too late. I have stepped on a patch of smashed pumpkin, and I slip on a heap of squash and seeds. Canned pasta and frozen waffles and marshmallow cookies fly out into the street. I gather them up, imagining the evening exactly as it will unfold: how my mother and I will sit in the dark in our living room, afraid to turn on the lights or even the television, listening to the approaching feet of eager trick-or-treaters, and the hollow ding of the doorbell, and the shuffling and chatter and the eventual disappointed retreat of those who are turned away unsatisfied.

James Woodfin, the Suicidal Maniac: This was his official title at Brown High School. Last year James had snuck into the garage of his house at three o'clock on a Saturday morning, doused his shirt in gasoline, and lit a match. His burns were severe. He had crawled back into his house, half-blind, and struggled down the long, dark hallway to his parents' room. When the police and ambulance and fire department came it woke the whole neighborhood. We stood in doorways with our arms folded in the glare of the red and blue lights of five emergency vehicles. Many of us assumed that James's father, Mr. Woodfin, had at last suffered a heart attack. He was a pink-faced man with a bulging stomach and a flair for violent outbursts. Hourly Mr. Woodfin could be heard cursing the family dog, a giant dalmation, who liked to stand in the Woodfin's backyard, on their picnic table, facing the house, barking loudly and rhythmically for hours on end. "Jesus Christ, Dildo," Mr. Woodfin would yell. "Shut the fuck up, you spotted sack of shit!" No one suspected that James, the Woodfins' only child, would have done something so noteworthy. For years he had lived in that house, and shuffled through our town's public schools, and delivered the morning paper at five o'clock each weekday morning, buzzing through the neighborhood on his moped—for years he had done all of this in nearly complete silence. No one knew him.

James was friendless, and therefore the victim of rumors. Some said that James was in the habit of cutting himself every time he fought with his parents, and that his chest was like a quilt. Others claimed to have seen James walking alone in the city, late at night, in dangerous and suggestive proximity to groups of streetwalkers in their fishnet stockings and ratty fox stoles, all of whom were making a better living than the rest of us. The only thing we knew for sure about James was that he was tall and lanky and gray-eyed, that he kept his black hair long enough that it covered his eyes, and that he stuttered. He had suffered horribly in grade school. When he was forced to answer a question in class, he would grip the edges of his desk, and his head would jerk. Veins bulged in his neck, and his eyes would roll back. Eventually, in our childish versions of politeness, we simply stopped speaking to James.

Because I was James's next-door neighbor, I knew something of his life at home. I knew that Mr. Woodfin was ashamed of his son, that he yelled at James most evenings, telling him to be a man, for Christ's sake, just once in his rotten miserable life. "Wha-wha-wha-wha-*what* did you say?" Mr. Woodfin mocked, every so often, when

James stormed out of the house, letting the screen door slam. "You can go fa-fa-fa-fa-*fuck* yourself!" I never told anyone in our class about Mr. Woodfin, about James's suffering. I wondered if he knew that I kept his secret, if he thought of me at all.

And so in a surprising and brilliant protest to his father, his hometown, his isolation, James had lit himself on fire. When school started up in the fall, James began the year as though nothing had happened. He walked the halls with impeccable posture, his head held high, gazing dreamily past the stares of his classmates. In class he sat up straight and took notes in a tiny, intricate script. The only thing different about James that year was that every day he wore a black trench coat and combat boots, which did a good job of hiding his scars. But he couldn't entirely cover his neck, which was pink and wrinkled, like worms, and he couldn't hide his face, the red, oval-shaped patches, like slices of roast beef, that had been grafted to his cheeks.

It wasn't until Halloween, when James dressed as a ghost, when his white bedsheet brushed against my shoulder on the walk home from the grocery, that James displayed the slightest strange behavior. On the day after Halloween, James showed up to school in his costume. Our teachers pretended not to notice the ghost sitting up perfectly straight in their classrooms, taking detailed notes. A week passed. We admitted to no discomfort when the ghost, already so far out of season, passed us in the hall. James could see us without being seen. Whatever regrets we suffered over James and his solitary life, the agony that we developed and carried around in our minds, even our dreams—this was the revenge of the meek, the lonely, the dead.

Weekday afternoons I return home to the madness of my mother's illegal day-care service. She keeps two neighborhood children while their parents are at work. Maxwell, a blond, plump terror whose parents both work at McDonald's, can be heard yelling a hundred yards from the house.

"Sandy, Sandy," he says, this day like any other. "The beach is home."

"Sandy the Beach!" cries my mother. It is her clever pet name, her underhanded and diabolical version of humor.

"Hello, Lydia. Hello, Maxwell," I say, hunched miserably under a backpack full of books. I have walked home through rain in soggy shoes, sniffling, wiping my nose with my mitten. I am playing for sympathy.

"Maxwell has something to tell you," my mother says, placing her hand on his blond head.

"Sorry, Sandy. Sorry, sorry, sorry, sorry, sorry."

"Sorry for what?"

"For your room," he says, and giggles maniacally, turning his face into the skirt of my mother's housecoat.

"I couldn't stop him," my mother calls after me. "He's an animal!"

I have seen worse. In my room, for the hundredth time, I find drawers pulled out from the dresser, underwear flung about, socks separated from their happy marriages. My bed, which I straighten and tuck every morning with military precision, is stripped of its blankets. The fine tips of my sharpened pencils, which I keep in a mug on my desk, have been snapped off. Worst of all, I find my aloe plant overturned and oozing, its soil scattered on the carpet.

"I'm going to kill you, you little shit," I call, stomping out to the kitchen, where I find another round of absurdity. Pilar—the six-month-old baby whose parents are first-year surgical residents at the city hospital, parents who drop her off at four in the morning and pick her up at midnight—Pilar is screaming in her high chair. Maxwell stands before her with one of my childhood teddy bears, Benjy. "Baby, baby, baby, baby," Maxwell says, making the bear talk in a squealing voice, thrusting it in Pilar's face. "Poor little foreign baby!" My mother is nowhere to be found.

"Quit it, Maxwell," I say, grabbing the bear out of his hands. But the baby is beyond repair. She has the scream of a bald eagle. I move to stroke her hair but she flinches, screams even louder.

"Okay, Pilaf," my mother says, suddenly appearing. "Don't cry. Only a few more years of this and your parents will be rich." My mother takes the baby from her high chair, and she calms. She clings to my mother's chest, latches on to my mother's housecoat with clenched fists. My mother is Pilar's mother, more so than anyone wants to admit. Pilar's parents are at the hospital so much that the baby has ceased to react when they pick her up. "Where's my girl?" Pilar's mother says each night, all excitement. But Pilar sits nonchalantly in her chair, yawning. It is too embarrassing to stand. Pilar's mother thrusts a wad of cash into my mother's hand, gathers her baby, leaves without another word.

"Let's make you some bacon," my mother tells the baby. My mother has been forbidden to feed the baby meat, and doing so is her secret joy.

"Mom," I say. "You're not supposed to."

"She loves it!" my mother says. "You know, you're turning into a real drag, Sandy. You're more like your father every day." My mother takes Benjy from my hands and turns him on me. "Let's see some more Mozart," she has the bear say to me. "Less Beethoven."

My mother was a music teacher at the local junior high for fifteen years, but she lost her job after a series of layoffs in which all teachers of supplemental subjects, such as art and music, were let go. Only the essential faculty remained, including gym instructors. The gym teachers—recent graduates of junior colleges—kept their jobs with full benefits, an irony that made the already significant torture of playing indoor dodgeball even worse.

My mother has grown strange in the months since she lost her job. She spends her free time in our damp, unfinished basement watching television and eating entire bags of Pecan Sandies. The smell of them is always on her breath, their crumbs caught in the folds of her clothes. On rainy afternoons she is fond of turning up the volume full blast on her organ and playing the kinds of frightening chords popular in vampire movies. They shake the house in bursts. Each time I hear one I see a vision of my mother as Dracula, spinning around to face me, her teeth bared, a cape flapping magnificently behind her. Lately my mother even dresses gloomily, in a black velour housecoat. Her hair, which had been dyed black for years but which is now almost entirely gray, hangs wearily down her back. She is defeated. Music had been her life. She was the kind of music teacher who wrote letters on special stationary that was lined with G clef staffs. She dotted the "i" in her name, Lydia, with an eighth note.

In my mother's opinion the world is filled with and ruled by idiots. Her defeat in this situation, knowing that she is hopelessly outnumbered, has had the effect of almost entirely silencing her. Her only friends are children. In public she barely speaks, and suffers insults without protest. She sighs when the supermarket clerk gyps her out of an advertised sale price, sighs when propositions pass that she has voted against, sighs when happy, youthful couples walk past us in the mall, we the jilted wife and daughter of a luckless raconteur. Only now and then her wit slips out, a sign of protest. Every so often she mutters asides under her breath, like W. C. Fields. "Never give a sucker an even break," she is fond of saying. Or, "Children should be neither seen nor heard."

The longer my father is gone, without sending money or even a word of his whereabouts, the more my mother and I grow sheepish, awkward, strange. Some days now my mother will only speak to me with the help of an inanimate translator, Benjy. Benjy's fur is matted, mangy. His body is flattened in places and bulging in others, his stuffing having shifted under the force of gravity and the occasional pile of books he has been trapped under for weeks at a time. Benjy is also marked by the drool and gnawing of Pilar and Maxwell. One of his eyes, a brown button, hangs miserably from a thin thread. My mother likes to wave the bear playfully while it talks. It only speaks in an exaggerated girly voice, like Betty Boop. *"Oooh,"* Benjy says, when I come home from school, "Mommy's *late.* And she looks like she's in a *bad mood.*" I glare at the bear whenever it speaks to me, and try to rip it from my mother's hands.

Sometimes I grab it by the throat and throw it on the floor, step on its back. "Don't hurt me!" the bear screams. The bear's chief complaint is that I am leaving for college in a few months, and it wants to come along. "Oh, no, Mommy," the bear is fond of saying, "I'm *naked*! I need some new clothes for school."

The closer I come to leaving for college, the more my mother takes refuge in the bear. Lately she has begun caring for it like a baby, like her second child, sitting him in a high chair next to the dinner table, extending forkfuls of potatoes and green beans to its mouth before taking a bite herself, having long conversations with the bear, making it proclaim its everlasting love and devotion for her, taking it to bed, brushing its fur, and ironing each morning one of a whole wardrobe of satin ribbons to be tied around its neck, and, bothered by its dangling eye, buying and altering a pirate's patch to slant across its head.

"More Mozart, less Beethoven," the bear says again.

"Mom!" I say, but she won't look at me. She waves the bear tauntingly in my face.

"She's not talking to you," says the bear. "I am."

Though it is raining, and nearly dark, I walk out to the backyard and take shelter in my father's slanting tool shed. The shed is poorly made out of old, rotting lumber, and there are wide gaps between the boards. My father's tools hang from hooks. A shovel and a rake lean in one corner. There is a shelf on the back wall, stacked with rolls of duct tape, paintbrushes, jugs of turpentine and gasoline, and old coffee cans filled with nails and bolts. Also on the shelf is a pack of my father's cigarettes, Lucky Strikes. I take the cigarettes and hold them up to my nose, wanting some memory of my father, but the smell is faint.

I drop the cigarettes when I hear the scurry of a rodent at my feet. It is a small brown field mouse, no more than three inches long. Its whiskers twitch. Merciless, petty, I grab the shovel from its corner and bring it down on the mouse, wishing, before I am even through with my swing, that I had walked away and left it alone. I consider leaving the mouse on the floor of the shed, its head flattened, bloody, and unrecognizable. But I go out into the rain, into our dark patch of back lawn, and dig a hole by the fence behind the shed. When I finish burying the mouse I stand over its grave, leaning on the handle of the shovel. I try to concentrate on a kind thought to help usher the mouse from this earth—a comforting verse about nature or the food chain or reincarnation as a higher entity, perhaps a squirrel. But I am aware, dreadfully, of a faint scraping a few feet away, in the Woodfin's yard. When I turn to look I see a blur of white, a ghost bent over his yard work. James is raking the lawn in the rain. He works slowly, methodically, gathering the wet leaves together in small piles. I face James and raise my hand up, and keep it there, as though taking an oath. I don't know if James sees me or not, for he gives no sign. The rainfall is heavy, and James's sheet clings to him. He is rail thin, a ghost of a ghost. I wonder if he feels the rain on his skin, the cold, or if his scars have dulled for him even the sensation of moving through weather, through space, through time.

We are behind the times, this failed industrial city. Our factories are empty, useless, outdated. We produce nothing. Our only functioning facility is a state-of-the-art trash incinerator, perched atop a high hill. A dozen counties send their garbage here. Their trucks, giant donkeys burdened with trash, grumble past out houses, gears grinding, brakes wailing, toward the incinerator, where a flame rumored to burn at eighteen hundred degrees swallows tons of garbage a day, a flame so fierce, we're told, that it can reduce a sofa to a handful of ashes in under thirty seconds, and so well engineered that the smoke it releases through the stacks—though black—is entirely refined of pollutants. The smoke rises and swirls, rises and swirls, all day, stretching out over our houses, darkening our windows with the ashy remnants of the unwanted—the sleeper sofas, dining room tables, kitchen appliances, tennis rackets, encyclopedia sets, LPs, patent leather shoes, photo albums, and board games of our friends and neighbors.

My neighborhood is settled in a valley between two small hills—one the site of our infamous incinerator, and one the site of White City, a commercial sprawl, acres of neon, a collection of the city's best resources—gas stations, grocery stores, ice-cream parlors, pizza places, tire and lube and muffler garages, windowless government offices, donut shops, and vocational high schools. This is a neighborhood of two-bedroom, single-bath homes with wood-paneled walls and unfinished basements. Each plot of land is bordered by a chain-link fence. It is a neighborhood populated by plumbers, carpenters, truck drivers, telephone operators, cashiers, bank tellers, fast-food restaurant managers, and retired military men. There is a hunched hatchback or a shamelessly hulking station wagon in every driveway. And on nearly every set of cold, crumbling front steps there is a man staring down into a coffee mug, steam circling slowly toward his face, or there is a man whittling with a jackknife, smoking a cigarette, or a man uprooting a political sign in his front yard, signs in favor of failed candidates who promised jobs, jobs, jobs, as full-time factory workers with benefits and dental, jobs as manufacturers of military equipment and nuclear weapons, state-funded jobs as policemen and firemen and construction workers. These are my neighbors, the men trying to escape the house. But having no money and nowhere to go, they choose the front steps and the chill of autumn. They have watched leaves change and fall, the grass wilt. They have been waiting for jobs since spring.

We, their children, wear the marks of their shame. We wear their palm prints. As teenagers we endure the humiliation of our parents, a sickness that can unleash itself at strange, unexpected moments. Our parents have drunkenly burst into our rooms late at night while we are sleeping, turning the lights on and ripping the covers from our beds, and have told us to get the hell up, start earning our keep in those godforsaken houses, and at three in the morning we have found ourselves scrubbing kitchen floors on our hands and knees, listening to our parents' stories of hardship, the brutal conditions they endured at our age. We fight back with silence and sarcasm, and have cigarettes put out on our backs. We are kicked in the pants, slapped across the face. And after we have scrubbed the floor or washed the dishes or shoveled the driveway or raked the leaves, our parents have cried to us, great miserable sobs of regret and apology, and what grows in us more than any other desire is the desire to sleep. To return to bed, the dark solitude of our small bedrooms, to sleep it off through the morning, through daylight, through the winter until the summer of our eighteenth year, the season of our imminent escape. We want to get out, to move on. We want, at the very least, to suffer somewhere else.

My father left after just such an evening. He had woken my mother and me at four in the morning and demanded we stand trial in the kitchen while he listed our offenses. He swayed in the kitchen's bright light, its yellow wallpaper, its yellow linoleum floor. His eyes were blurry and red, his hair slicked down on his forehead. He had walked home two miles through rain, sick and drunk. He had called us for a ride, goddamn it, fifty times if he'd called us once, and now his boots were waterlogged, ruined, like the love he had once carried for us blissfully, lightly, effortlessly, in his giant goddamned heart.

The next morning my father announced that he was taking me to his favorite place, the dog track. We sat in the bleachers among ruthless patrons, who threatened the dogs with beatings and even death if they didn't for Christ's sake run faster. We sat next to men in fedoras and polyester pants, men with stubby cigars and rotting teeth and bulging veins, men with thermoses full of whiskey, men who cried at the tops of their lungs for their number thirteen dog to run, goddamn it, for the sake of the rent, the leaking roof, the stalled car, to run for the sake of doubling their last severance check, for the sake of baby's perpetual new pair of shoes. Watching the dogs circle the track, I recognized for the first time a horrible truth about myself: that I had worn for sixteen years, without knowing it, the face of a greyhound. Bony and fierce, slight, with wet, bulging eyes, a long nose, and the expression of something recently beaten.

This was my face. The resemblance was so obvious to me that I grew sick with embarrassment, as though I were naked in front of the crowd. I asked to leave but my father insisted on dispensing advice. This was his fatherly swan song, though I didn't yet know of his plans to leave. He left me with a handful of harsh facts, most surprisingly the revelation that a pig going to market wasn't the same thing as a pig sent out with fifty bucks for the week's groceries.

He left that night, leaving behind only the gray suit bought for his father's funeral, which hangs now in the coat closet so far to the right that we usually forget it is there, with its useless buttons on the coat sleeve, three of them, matched with holes already sewn, never meant for a single moment to close a gap.

The time moves slowly. I am stuck forever in the middle of *Middlemarch*, the subject of my term paper. Our teacher requires us to compose a list of questions about the book, things that we would like to answer in a ten page essay. "Why is the main character so stupid?" I write. "Why doesn't she just book a seat on the next flight to Milwaukee?" Before turning in our drafts, we are each paired with another class member for peer review. James and I are assigned to one another. We sit in a corner of the classroom, a ghost and a hoax. He reads about my frustrations with Dorothea Brooke and George Eliot, about not knowing when to get out when the getting is good. James has written twenty-five pages on Dostoyevsky's *The Idiot*, and his paper is a brilliant treatise on the importance of outcasts. I write three pages of confession to James, unburdening myself, saying how I've always cared for him and wondered about him, asking him about his plans after graduation, offering to serve him coffee and ice cream for free if he ever wants to visit me at my job at Friendly's restaurant, weeknights from six to eleven.

I wait for James's reply. Thanksgiving comes and goes. I watch the Macy's parade with my mother and Pilar, both of them gnawing mercilessly on legs of turkey. Soon after, the first snow falls. The sky will remain cloudy, colorless, for the rest of winter. The black smoke clouds of the incinerator stand out best in this cold season. They seem to keep their shape in this weather, and seem always to float in the direction of our house.

I still wait for James's reply. I work nights and weekends at Friendly's, scooping ice cream and serving hamburgers, slogging through my shift without looking anyone in the eye. An autistic savant sits nightly in my section in a yellow rain slicker, drawing cathedrals on napkins and drinking cups of coffee loaded with sugar. Each night he leaves a scratch ticket on the table, as a tip, and each night I return home with luckless traces of silver under my nails. "Gramma and I waited for you to come home all day!" screams Benjy, when I walk through the door. "Where the hell have you *been*?" I give the bear the finger and head for my room. "Don't worry, Benjy," I hear my mother saying. "Gramma still loves you. Even if Mommy doesn't. Even if Mommy's turning into a snooty college bitch." My mother cradles the bear in her arms, and rocks it frantically.

I wait for James's reply. Finally, just before Christmas, our neighborhood is wakened once again by police sirens. I watch from my bedroom window as James, having lost a liter of blood after slitting his wrists, is carried from his house on a gurney, as short men in white uniforms lift him into the back of an ambulance. "Do you think he's dead?" I hear my mother say, her voice soft and blank. She is standing in my bedroom doorway. All I can see of her is the shining silver of her long hair. I realize that she could be talking about either James or my father. I realize it is the first time she has spoken to me, without the help of Benjy, in weeks.

James does not return to school after Christmas break. We are told that he is recovering at home, and finishing his coursework there. My English teacher reads James's paper on *The Idiot* to the class, her eyes brimming with tears. She looks up from the paper now and then, staring at us accusatorily. She repeats the final para-

graph of the paper three times, so that we understand its importance. "We neglect the potential of our surroundings. These days
most of us are jewelers in search of flaws," James had written. "We
are in the habit of examining each gem through such a powerful
scope that we fail to see its beauty." I consider knocking on the
Woodfins' door that day after school, and every day afterward, but
I am deterred by the bark of their dalmation, by the sound of Mr.
Woodfin yelling, by the cheeriness of television advertisements
blaring in the living room. Sometimes I make it as far as the door,
my knuckles poised for knocking, before turning back. And sometimes I simply stand in the snow by the chain-link fence that sepa-
rates our yards, staring at James's house, at the dark window that
I suspect is his.

Spring: My mother decides to fill the circular above-ground pool in
our backyard. The pool has been empty for years, but my mother
now sees its potential as a kind of playpen. "I'll strap some floats on
those kids and let them splash around all day," she says. "I'll just sit
in the lawn chair eating cookies and reading magazines." But my
mother neglects to treat the pool, and its surface turns marshy. A
fine moss settles over the water, a tapestry of fungus and fallen leaves
and drowned insects. By the time it is warm enough to swim, the
pool is hopeless.

It is a season of indecision. I have won scholarships to two colleges after writing devastating personal essays about the economic
recession and its impact on families. I mention my poor, poor
mother, laid off from her life's work, and I mention the sad, longing
music she plays on her piano when she thinks no one is listening. I
mention my hard luck father, traveling the country looking for decent work, his skin so callused from hard labor that his potential
employers know from the first handshake that he is a man out of his
league. I have a choice between two schools, one in California and
one in my hometown, which my mother assumes I don't have the
gall to abandon.

I return home from one of my last days of school to the usual day-care circus.

"Quack, quack, quack," Maxwell says, flapping his arms and walking in circles around the kitchen.

"Quack," says Pilar, sitting as always in her high chair, sucking on a strip of bacon. Her brown eyes are beautiful, and always wet with tears.

"Quack," says my mother, appearing from the living room, where she has been watching soap operas. "My dear, there are baby ducks trapped in the pool. And we're going to watch you save them."

There are indeed five baby ducks trapped in the pool, too small to fly themselves to freedom. How they made it into the pool is a mystery. Regardless, they have been swimming in circles for hours, possibly days, without stopping. I hear their mother quacking somewhere in the yard. "She's been doing that for hours," says my mother. "If I had a gun I'd shoot her."

"Kill her, kill her, Benjy," cries Maxwell, and he runs off in search of the mother, making the bear growl.

The idea is for me to lean over the side of the pool, reach out with my arms, and usher the ducks into a large pot. I move for them, but they circle away. I lean farther in, balancing on my stomach. I can see the birds' tiny feet moving under the water, precise and rhythmic. The mother honks miserably. I hear her coming closer, and then all at once there is a flurry of wings, and she is flying straight for my face. I lose my balance and fall headfirst into the pool, into the filth and slime that has collected there for weeks. My mother, Maxwell, and Pilar are thoroughly entertained. Chest-high in filth, I gather the ducks into the pot, climb out, and release them. They strut away behind their mother, nonchalant.

"I hate you," I yell at my mother, who is still laughing. "And I hate you," I tell Maxwell. "I hate everyone in this whole town and I hope you all die." It is the first time I have raised my voice to my mother. She takes Benjy from Maxwell and chases me into the house. "Oh, no," cries the bear. "Poor Mommy needs some *anger management.* Maybe Mommy should get some *professional help.*"

"Fuck off!" I tell the bear, swatting at it.

"Oh, no," says the bear. "Mommy smells like a *hooker!*"

I decide that day to commit to California. I walk to the nearest mailbox, pull at its moaning door, and mail my acceptance. I decide not to tell my mother, to let her continue to believe that I plan to enroll in our city's pitiful satellite to our state university.

All summer James fails to emerge from his house. I watch for him, spend time lurking by the fence in the backyard, but he never appears. Once I desperately called out to Mrs. Woodfin, who was hanging clothes on the line, asking if she wanted me to trim back the branch of one of our trees that extended into her yard.

"What?" she said, turning toward me. Her gray hair was set in curlers, her feet tucked in slippers.

"How's James?" I called.

"What?" she said, cupping her hand behind her ear. She was utterly surprised to be spoken to, and looked at me with fear, as if I were a talking bear.

"Nothing," I said. "Never mind."

A week before I was to board the Greyhound for college, I received a letter from my father, who always had a knack for timing. He wrote that he was in a rehabilitation center in New Hampshire, recovering from a stroke. He wrote how strange it was to lounge around all day with nothing but thoughts for company. He wrote he was sorry. He wrote he had worked his whole life at tough jobs, lumberjack, butcher, and now he was stuck there in the unfamiliar stiffness of clean sheets. He asked to be visited, and included a list of contraband indulgences I might bring along. Cigarettes, a fifth of Jack. He also complained that he missed the pleasure of sucking meat off chicken wings. He missed the sight of a pile of small, helpless bones on his plate after each meal. In closing, my father mentioned the daily torture of a blinking neon sign visible from his bedroom window. COLD ICE CREAM, it read. What he wouldn't do for a milkshake.

"If you can't come see me it's okay," he wrote. "Although I do miss having a radio, which you could bring me."

That night, after work, I undressed and stood in front of my mirror. I was a mess. So thin, all ribs and hip bones, and so pale. My skin was bluish-white, like skim milk. There was ice cream smeared on my arms and face. I hadn't noticed any of this, hadn't really looked at myself in months.

"Sandy," someone called, in a loud and sure and commanding voice. Someone was in the backyard. I went to the window, pressed my face against the screen, squinted.

"Good-bye," said the voice. And then I saw a slight figure, retreating into darkness.

"James!" I called. "Wait!" I pulled on a T-shirt and ran from the house into the yard. "James!"

What took me by surprise at first was the smell, an overwhelming sweetness, like I was walking through a grove of grapefruit trees. And then from the corner of my eye I saw a burst of brightness. It was the pool. It was its usual four-foot-tall circle, but the dark water was gone, the horrible smell of rot, the mass grave of spiders and crickets, the layer of scum mixed with fallen leaves, all of that was gone. The pool was choked with flowers. James had floated dozens of flower blossoms on the surface of the water. I took one in my hands and held it, brought it to my nose, took in its sweet, sweet smell. I imagined James spending the afternoon in better neighborhoods, stealing through private gardens. He must have collected the blossoms in a sack, then floated them one by one in the pool's dark water. It must have taken him hours.

These were the first flowers I had ever received. I stood, staring at them for a long time, hoping that James would return. When he failed to emerge from the darkness as I had imagined it, as I had seen happen in films, I thought about knocking on his door, but it was too late. Tomorrow, I said.

James left the next day. I was still asleep when he loaded his suitcases into his parents' car and drove off with them. I had no idea where he had gone. A week later I walked to the bus station, leaving a note for my mother with my new address and phone number. "Call me in a week," it read. "Love, Sandy the Beach." The last I saw of my mother, she was slouched in her armchair, staring vacantly at the television, one hand buried inside a bag of Pecan Sandies.

After a month of college, when I finally decide to call home, Benjy answers. "Hello?" he cries, more Betty Boop than ever.

"Hi, Mom," I say.

"It's my mommy!" cries Benjy. "We've been waiting and waiting by the phone!"

"Mom?" I say.

"She's not home," says Benjy. "She's out on a hot date." There's something in Benjy's voice, a new enthusiasm, that sounds truly crazed, as if Benjy has wandered off too far from my mother's mental leash, never to return.

"Mom," I say. "What if it wasn't me calling? And you answered the phone like that?"

"I said she's *not home,*" says Benjy. "Cripes! So you'll never guess who called looking for you!"

"Who?" I ask, thinking of my father.

"I guess the Navy thinks it's okay to enlist *suicidal maniacs,*" says the bear.

"James called? He really called me? From the *Navy?* Did you give him my number?"

"Yes. And don't get so excited," says Benjy. "He's sailing the South Seas, a million miles away. It's not like he called for a date. Besides, what am I, chopped *liver?*" This is classic Benjy, one of his favorite questions.

"No. *I'm* a chopped liver," I say. "James is a chopped liver."

"What the hell are you talking about?" Benjy demands.

"Nothing," I say. "Forget it."

"How's school?" says Benjy. "Do you hate it? Do you miss me?"

"Well...," I say.

"Yes?" says Benjy.

"Can you keep a secret?"

"Can I? Of course I can!"

"Don't tell my mother," I say.

"Never!"

"Okay. Here goes...." I pause.

"Tell me!" cries Benjy. "I can't take the suspense!"

"The secret is that all her worst predictions are true...." I pause again.

"What do you mean?"

"I mean I love it here and I'm never coming back." For once, Benjy says nothing. "I have a million friends. And I'm so busy giving blow jobs to professors that I can't see straight."

"Shut up!" Benjy screams. "Don't say that. Just shut up!" Benjy is hysterical now, like a girl in a slasher movie.

"Mom?" I say. "Talk to me." A group of girls wanders by, headed to the lounge. They are dressed in pajamas and head scarves, and they are dissecting each other's strategies for sorority rush. They walk past without looking at me. I am huddled deep in the dark phone booth, the glass door pulled shut. There is such a long silence that I think I might have been cut off. The girls pass, and I hear their laughter trailing off.

"Talk to me, Mom," I say. "Please."

"She's not home," says Benjy, in a girly whisper. "I told you a million times."

Sometimes we miss our connections. We run frantically after busses, hailing them, knowing the driver sees us growing smaller in his mirror. When James finally called me, a few weeks later, I ran down the hallway to the phone booth. I was the only person who used that phone, for the rest of the girls on the hall had phones in their rooms. The ringing was fierce. When I answered the line there was only a strange humming. "Hello?" I said again, and waited. Just as I went to hang up I heard my name, faint and mechanical, followed by a click. "James?" I said.

"It's ship-to-shore," said a voice, followed by another click.

"What?"

"Ship-to-shore." Came the answer, five seconds later.

"James? Where are you?" I said.

"Don't say anything," said a voice, after a pause. It sounded faintly like James. "I want to see you. Can I see you?" Every time James spoke, the sound of his voice was followed by static. I couldn't tell when to speak. There was a long silence. "You're my only friend in the world," said James, and then the line was taken over with squeals.

"James!" I said. "Yes. Please." But the line was dead.

Our conversation was strangled by the strange technology of ship-to-shore, which I hadn't understood. We spoke over each other's words, impatient to be heard and answered. Something had cut us off, some loose wire, some crashing wave, and we never spoke again.

Weeks later I received a newspaper clipping from my mother. It was James's obituary. He had swallowed a bottle of sleeping pills, on a ship somewhere in the Pacific. The newspaper had printed a picture of James in uniform. He wore a stoic expression under his ocean liner–shaped cap. I could just barely see his features, his scars.

I knew that James had died without ever hearing my answer, that I wanted to see him. I knew that we might have saved each other. Instead James had escaped, had simply fallen asleep, tucked in his bunk, lulled by waves. When I thought of him I choked, wondering about that dark, narrow corner in which he died, and whether he was calm, or scared, or lonely. Or perhaps, finally, at peace.

There was no escape for me. I thought constantly of James. I thought of my mother, who I imagined playing her organ late into the night, or absently stroking Benjy's fur, staring at the television. I thought of my father half-paralyzed in a nursing home, looking out the window, expecting someone, wanting a milkshake, wanting a radio. It was nearly impossible to bear, this burden of adulthood, which James had understood all his life. Sooner or later, finding ourselves alone, we all came to appreciate the importance of outcasts.

Take Them In, Please

The daughter is leaving home, and the time has come for advice, so the mother tells the story of how she once fought off a high-school-state-champion wrestler in the back seat of his Chevy by holding the blade of her ice skate to his temple. The mother and the wrestler had just spent an hour gliding around the local pond with other young couples. They enjoyed those quaint comforts that hadn't the strength to survive through the daughter's time: tie-on skates with leather straps, roasted chestnuts, five-cent cocoa served from the back of an old woman's station wagon. And then the wrestler had tugged the mother to the far edge of the pond, where the ice was nearly transparent, unetched by blades. The mother heard the faintest creaking under her feet, imagined the impression of a fish gliding past, a shadow of its trailing fin. The mother had been offered advice about falling through: If trapped under ice and unable to locate the hole through which one fell, look for the light. If unable to find the light, swim to the surface and raise one's lips to the ever-so-thin layer of air between ice and water, a small gap that may save an intelligent life. Breathe slowly and carefully through the mouth.

This advice for free. But nothing about a wrestler's fat fingers, the pinch and snap of cotton tights against the thigh, the fumbling at the hem of a pleated wool skirt, the scuff of chapped lips, the desperate flop of mittens clipped to the jacket cuff. And so the mother, without advice, held up the toe of the skate blade, which was jagged for the purposes of braking.

The mother now wishes to recreate the scene for her daughter. For flair, she pulls a grapefruit spoon from the silverware drawer. "So I held that skate right up to his temple," she says, with fisted spoon. She makes a vicious face and assaults the father, who is seated at the kitchen table awaiting breakfast, who is frowning at the sports page, who bats away the grapefruit spoon and clasps the short juice glass in which floats his daily raw egg. Tilt of the head and one swallow, the thick yolk rolling down his throat, a glossy rim of albumen around his lips. He gives a phlegmy clearing of the throat. Swipe of the hand across the mouth, his ruined knuckles swollen to the size of gumballs. "That's when I knew your mother was for me," he says, still intent on the paper, the slim and tragic wrestling column.

More advice the mother could have used: It is acceptable to name a child after a warm and inviting month. April, May, June. Days of the week are another story. A name at once unusual and mundane. *Wednesday*. Sandwiched, too easily given to the influence of its surroundings.

Morbid proof: For a few years during Wednesday's girlhood, the six o'clock news runs a weekly report called *Wednesday's Child*, which advertises adolescents in desperate need of adoption. Every week there's another mumbling boy, slouching in his Celtics sweatshirt, answering the reporter's questions.

"What's your name?"

"Michael."

"How old are you?"

"Thirteen."

"Why are you a Wednesday's Child?"

"I don't know. Because I have no place to live."

Wednesday's children are never adopted. They grow up under the care of the state, and enter adulthood in desperate need of practical advice: how to polish a shoe, conquer a stain, how to stack a sandwich, how to file a complaint, how to introduce oneself to strangers, how to get home if lost.

Walk softly, carry a sharp skate. Wednesday heads by train to Louisville with this advice and two pieces of luggage. The first, a backpack stuffed with a week's supply of T-shirts, underwear, and Saltine crackers. The second, a three-foot-tall cardboard box that the wrestler has brought home from the Dumpster of King's Meatpacking, his place of employ. The box is marked with wobbly red stains of dribbled blood. The wrestler has strangled the box with silver tape, and fashioned a slim handle from a wire coat hanger. He has printed neatly on three-by-five index cards, and taped one to each side of the box: FRAGILE, DELICATE CONTENTS, THIS END UP, DO NOT OPEN UNTIL SETTLED IN LOUISVILLE. The box is awkward but light. It is entirely possible that the box is empty, the latest in a long line of the father's characteristically last minute, hopelessly flimsy gestures. The daughter stores the box underneath her feet, thinks nothing of its contents. She is busy with a mock southern accent, thoughts of white riverboats propelled by giant red paddles, the difference between bourbon and whiskey, the proportions of a mint julep. She is busy with thoughts of her boyfriend, who has moved to Louisville for his first year of medical school, and rented an apartment for next to nothing because it is an unfurnished loft above a hardware store owned by a man who has legally changed his name to Jack Hammer, and because it is also twelve feet away from the intersection of train tracks and a major thoroughfare.

Wednesday has dropped out of school, where she has performed only just well enough to keep her scholarship, and followed the medical student to Louisville because he is what her family has called a first-class ticket, not to be surrendered to the hardships of geography. Because he is a brief four years away from the white coat, the prescription pad, the crabbed writing and dangling, cold stethoscope, the rushed rustle of crisp-seamed slacks. She follows him because she has never spent a night away from her parents' house, an arrangement that she feels has deprived her of the illicit joys of college life. More than all of these things, she follows him because during their two-year acquaintance he played the cello in a college rock band, because he sat on stage with his eyes closed, swiping his bow across the strings, producing not one sound loud enough to hear.

Although she can't be sure, Wednesday assumes that the medical student welcomes her south because she has charmed him over the past two years with her ability to publicly improvise, in great detail, at bars and in elevators, the most outlandish stories about her personal involvement in globally significant scandals: her love affair with Fidel Castro, her hitchhiking trip across country at the age of fifteen with a series of grandfatherly truckers, with names like Buttsy and Giorgio, any of whom may have been Jimmy Hoffa in disguise. In any situation—at a gallery opening or a funeral—Wednesday is able to enthrall a crowd. It is a peculiar gift for a shy person to bear.

When Wednesday's train arrives in Louisville, the medical student is waiting at the station, sitting in a folding metal chair, the cello between his legs. She sees him through the short train window, and he is there on the platform scanning the crowd, fingers poised on the cello strings, waiting to begin. The longing for that sound. She fits her arms through her backpack and hurries down the narrow aisle, its threadbare red carpet.

The apartment is a one-room rambling loft with splintery hardwood floors. The medical student has arranged, at random angles, a mattress on the floor, a television at the foot of the bed, and two orange beanbag chairs. The furniture is like the inadequate clothing of gingerbread men, two or three spheres of candy meant to suggest buttons. Buttons without a shirt. The bathroom is a stand-up shower and a toilet walled off in one corner. There is a sink and a stove, and a back door leading out to a porch without railings.

The apartment was last occupied by a seamstress, who had placed handmade signs in the two front windows, facing the street. Block letters on white paper: TAKE THEM IN, PLEASE. LET THEM OUT, THANK YOU. The medical student leaves the signs up for Wednesday's arrival, then sets them out with the trash in the back alley. But the following morning, at the high yawning sound of the garbage truck, Wednesday runs out and retrieves the signs, returns them to their places. "Take them in, please," she says. "Let them out." The medical student indulges her, since it is a strange city with little amusement. He crouches to read the section of newspaper that is unfolded on the floor. He frowns at the circled classifieds. Wanted: Companion to elderly gentleman. Requires heavy cleaning with harsh solvents. Wanted: Experienced dancers for exclusive gentlemen's club. Fifty-thousand annual potential.

Wednesday receives her first letter at her new address. It is a rare occasion, something to be savored. For flair, she opens the letter with a steak knife.

> *Dear Wednesday:*
>
> *You're probably wondering why I sent you off to your new life with an old clock. I wanted to explain and write it down but there wasn't time before you left. You left all of a sudden. It has taken me a lot of tries to get this letter right. But I figure better late than never.*
>
> *This clock was your great-uncle Eddy's. Uncle Eddy lived with me and my parents and my brothers. When he worked, he was a butcher like me. He was also a drunk and this clock was the only thing he didn't pawn or gamble for booze. He was a real gentleman who never spoke unless spoken to. When we ate*

dinner and someone said anything to Uncle Eddy he put down
his fork and answered and he wouldn't eat again until everyone
had stopped looking at him. I can't explain how he looked when
people talked to him. He was so nervous. He chewed on the
inside of his mouth. One time he came to a wrestling match of
mine. There weren't too many people there usually, and he stuck
out like a sore thumb. He wore bow ties, and he always had his
shoes shined and his shirts ironed, which is funny for a butcher.
He had very good posture. And I could tell he would never
wrestle anyone. Not that he couldn't. It was the thought of
touching another person. You could tell it made him sick. That
happens to guys sometimes in my profession. They don't want to
touch people anymore. Anyway, we used to have a piano in the
living room and there were sliding doors you could shut and be
alone in the room. He used to go in there and play music at
night. If you asked him in the morning what it was he was
playing, he walked away and said he didn't know how to play
piano. He'd look at you like you were crazy. But he did play. He
made up his own tunes. He died broke when he was only forty-
eight. They put him in the drunk ward down at Memorial. The
nurses were tough broads but he loved them. He always loved
women. They were an exception for him. He used to pay women
to sit with him when he was sick and just talk, just tell him about
movies they went to and things they wanted to buy. But that's
when and how he died. He was absolutely yellow when he died.
You've never seen anything like it. He had his clock with him in
the room because he liked to hear it chime. So that's a little bit
about my family since you always were asking. Great, right?
You're from a family of drunks and butchers. All the same, the
clock's yours now. I never wanted to have it out because I'd
break it. Be careful with it. It's worth something.

   Regards,
   Your father

The clock is snug in its box, strangled in silver tape, slid beneath a cushioned train seat, forgotten, rattling south and north. Or the clock is unpacked and chiming in a stranger's house.

There is no going home, now. The story of the clock is the first Wednesday's father has ever told her, and she has lost it. Still holding the steak knife, she makes a quick, angry slice at the arch of her foot, its shiny, unscuffed skin. A cut that bleeds and bleeds.

Now in Wednesday's life, keeping the time, there is the train and its accessory, the twenty-foot-high, red-and-white-striped traffic arm that blinks and dings every thirty minutes. Cars stop and line in front of the hardware store, the bass of their radio music booming so loud Wednesday feels it in her rib cage as she lies on the mattress on the floor. And the overzealous train driver gives long pulls at the chain horn, a high note of fear that she is forced to endure as the medical student–cello player sleeps soundly, a mouth-breather. He is not a wrestler or a drunk but a dignified sipper of Earl Grey, wearer of a blue cardigan with smooth wooden buttons on dangerously loose threads. His cello is leaning against the wall in its thin leather jacket, towering over the phone, which is kept, like everything else, on the floor. The phone rings exactly then, while Wednesday is looking at it, as though she had willed it. The phone is an old black rotary with a smooth fabric cord. The handle is heavy.

"Hello?" she says.

"Hello. What're your rates?"

"What?"

"This is Executive Escorts, right? It says here."

"No."

"Oh."

And not a minute later the phone again. "Executive Escorts," she says. The man hears her voice and is confused. He is calling, surely, from the basement bedroom of his mother's house with a three-year-old phone book balanced on his lap in which appears an impressive three-by-five advertisement for Executive Escorts, featuring models, models, models. He has called the same number twice and Wednesday has answered twice in her soft voice. "What're your rates?" he asks again, a little sheepish.

"A hundred dollars an hour, cash." At this and only this, instead of the passing train and the fierce ringing of the phone, the medical student awakens.

"Who are you talking to?" he says.

"Some guy. He says this is the phone number for an escort service."

"Hang up."

She hangs us and takes the phone off the hook. No getting back to sleep. There is the minute-long bleat of the phone line falling dead, and then eventually the train coming through again, the two-tone ding of the traffic arm. There is just enough time to run out on the back porch and wait for the train conductor who, if facing the right direction, will pass at eye level in his high cab and wave, they always wave, sometimes even remove their caps, if she waits shoe-less on the back porch, the splintery wood and flaking paint, the cut in her foot still open.

The medical student learns something new each day. Wednesday comes home one evening and is told about the six-feet-in-all-directions spray of fecal bacteria that spreads every time one flushes the toilet. The medical student explains that they must clear all possessions from the bathroom. The towels will be washed and stored in the empty kitchen cabinets. "We are filthy animals," he says.

The next morning Wednesday finds the toothbrush holder nailed to the wall by the front door, the brushes dangling like executed traitors.

Three weeks after Wednesday's arrival, the medical student quotes, over supper, a survey conducted by the National Institute for Health. It seems there is staggering evidence connecting work and well-being. If Wednesday fails to secure meaningful employment it is almost safe to assume that she will die of a major illness before the year's end.

"How about waitressing?" the medical student suggests. "You can tell wild stories to all your customers."

The next day Wednesday notices a sign in the window of a bar across the street. It is the kind of bar that requires employees to wear white shirts and colorful ties, though the shirts are floppy and wrinkled, bearing the ghosts of old stains, and the ties hang, loose and miserable, dipping into bowls of soup. Wednesday asks for the manager and he appears, an exceedingly short man with thin, cornsilk hair. If he were any less ferocious looking, Wednesday could not resist picking him up and sitting him on the bar like a child. But the manager's face looks as though it were stitched together from scraps.

"You're a tall drink of water," the manager says, sliding his hand under his tie, into the gap between the buttons of his shirt.

"Yeah," Wednesday says. Her voice is high and unsure, and the manager is pleased.

"Course, not me. I used to be a jockey, case you wondered. Good old Churchill." The manager smiles. His top front teeth are missing, and he runs a pointed tongue over his gums.

"Who?" says Wednesday.

"Churchill."

"A great man," says Wednesday. "So they say."

"The *Downs*?" says the manager. "The *Kentucky Derby*?"

"Oh. I just moved here."

"Jesus Christ. Sit down, have a seat, take a load off." The manager makes a slight bow. Wednesday sits on a swivel stool, its split red vinyl mended with silver tape. The manager remains standing, short of eye level. During the interview he picks at a bowl of assorted peanuts, and wipes his fingers discreetly on his tie. There are thin, colorless stitches tied in his cheeks and forehead, sticking out like whiskers.

"Just had some moles removed," the manager says, twisting the ends of a stitch together, just above his eyebrow. "Boy, I've been saving forever to do this." He twists away, dreamily, thinking of his new skin, forgetting that he is a short, balding manager of a bar that serves a daily lunch plate special of fried pork chops and peach chutney for two ninety-five.

Wednesday tells the manager the story of her life: how she was raised in Texas, the daughter of a butler who worked for a wealthy, globe-trotting oil mogul named Dallas Kincaid, whose phone number she cannot list for security reasons. But the manager should be assured that she can set an excellent table. And she certainly knows how to make a mint julep.

"Well, well," the manager says finally. "Welcome aboard." He removes his right hand from his face, where he has been fingering stitches. Wednesday takes his hand and agrees to start the next day, knowing that tomorrow, if her timing is right, dressed for work, she might instead hop a slow-moving train in search of her lost clock. A polka dot kerchief tied to a stick, stuffed with the wrestler's letter, and the loose pages of sheet music that the medical student has not played since the start of classes.

Again with the phone. Weeks upon weeks of late-night calls. Men, desperate and shy, wanting escorts. Angry men. Tired men. What are your rates? Wednesday answers the calls while the medical student sleeps soundly, dreaming of gross anatomy. He has seen the mechanics of human life, the traffic of blood, the filtering of toxins, and he has begun to think very little of the difference between any two men. The same urges from the same locations. They call and call. Men will never change. A hundred years ago, they sent the same messages by pony. *Please,* they say. *Talk to me.* They just want a sound in their motel rooms. Anything. A chime.

"You're not the only one with problems," Wednesday tells the man on the phone. "I'm a waitress. My feet hurt." It is a small, small step between waitress and escort. She considers this. The phone is on a long cord, and can be pulled out onto the back porch. It is four in the morning, and a small bird hops around the porch on its callused feet. Wednesday is still in her uniform, stained shirt and soup-splattered tie.

"I'll pay you," the man says. "Just talking. Just telling stories. With the money you take tomorrow off, rest your feet. Lucky Motel. Room 508."

The night watchman of the Lucky Motel is asleep in his glass booth, the neck of his shirt open, a gold cross gleaming on its chain. He wakes when the door chimes. "Sign in," he yells. But his voice is muffled through the glass. He points psychotically at the log, open on a tall lectern next to the door. Wednesday takes the pen and signs. *Take them in, please. Let them out, thank you.*

The light is yellow, the carpet red. Wednesday imagines the man waiting upstairs, drunk in his room. Sitting straight in his polished shoes, biting the inner corners of his mouth. They will talk. The sound of her voice will comfort him. He will thank her and casually pull enough money from his slim, oily wallet for a train ride home.

However unlikely, this is what she imagines.

Three Parting Shots and a Forecast

JOHN WILKES BOOTH

His Picture: A three-quarter shot, Booth leering just left of center, casual, as if turning toward someone who has called his name. No doubt a beautiful heiress, an adoring fan. He has a devil's ear, angled tight and sharp against his head, and his hair is brushed into nonchalant curls. Dark-eyed with eggshell skin, he wears a black moustache combed into a frown. At the time of the picture Booth is one of the most celebrated young actors in Washington City, and he dresses the part. He models a loose jacket, cut in the latest fashion, its collar and breast pocket trimmed with silk thread. The top button is fastened, and the rest of the jacket falls open in a triangle like a teepee. The pocket sprouts a starched handkerchief. His right hand, fat and smooth as a baby's, props a delicate bamboo walking stick. A small brass key dangles from his vest's middle button. (A remembrance? A safe-deposit box? The door to his room? No one is sure.) A gold ring wraps the little finger of his left hand, which grips the handle of something resembling a whip. He is a gentleman, a gentleman.

It is a good time for actors. The President himself attends the theater with some frequency. Theater-going is a pleasant diversion, and Lincoln's only opportunity to nap in peace. The President's box hovers twelve feet over stage left, and is about the size and shape of Lincoln's childhood log home. It seats four comfortably, five in a pinch. The President lounges in a distinctive rocking chair. It is one of Lincoln's favorite places, cozy and warm as a cradle.

Imagine, one evening, that Lincoln has trouble dozing off. A loony Hamlet trots underfoot. The actor's interpretation requires a certain amount of gymnastics. It is a promenade of leaping and screeching. "TO BE!" Booth booms, looks skyward, drops to one knee, rolls onto his back. "OR NOT TO BE!" He clutches the open neck of his shirt and howls. Booth turns a cartwheel and decides on the question. The crowd loves him. Perhaps they find his aerobics refreshing in such solemn times. What's a play these days, anyway, but a moment's distraction? Who wants to look death too plainly in the face?

The President decides to sleep out the rest of the performance, chin slumped on his chest. Just then, Booth steals a glance at the shadowed figure. Asleep! In the middle of his soliloquy! He stops for a moment, stumbles on the verse. Lincoln's legs are outstretched— propped on the banister—and the giant, scuffed soles of his shoes face the stage like twin hecklers. Imagine living under the reign of such an unmannered buffoon. Booth decides, then and there, to take some kind of action. Curiously, as the play wears on, Booth's performance improves. The audience remarks how distressed and convincing he is, as if he were really and truly at odds with an unrightful king.

Lincoln wakes rested as the lights come up. It is his best sleep in weeks.

There is little rest for Booth after his plan begins to materialize. During the first months of 1865, Booth dreams—nightly—his own set of tragedies. They take different forms. The worst of the lot occurs on stage. Just as he has the crowd in his grip, just as he works Hamlet or Romeo or King Lear into the most innovative and tortured interpretation of the century, the crowd howls with laughter. The gas lights jet up, flickering blue and then white. He sees people twisting in their chairs, the men clutching their stomachs, the women covering their faces with gloved hands. Booth checks to see that his fly is buttoned. "What?" he demands, stomping a foot. "Blast!" Booth likes to curse in the manner of all true southern gentleman—forcefully, but with restraint. The audience can't seem to get a hold of themselves. Booth storms toward the curtain, bats at it to split the seam so he can slip off stage. But the curtain is stitched together at its center, and only sways from the rafters like a bemused spirit. The theater takes on the look of a large carnivorous mouth, its domed ceiling like a palate. The wooden seats like false teeth, the audience rolling and flapping like a crazy tongue. They will swallow him. There is nothing to do but submit. Booth drops to one knee and makes the motions of a prayer—an act, but isn't everything?

Suddenly the audience calms. Booth hears his name announced from overhead, a high pitched and familiar voice, not quite human. "Booth," he hears again, and looks skyward. Lincoln stands in his elaborate box, tall as Goliath. He extends an arm toward the stage and turns his mouth into a wry smile.

Young man, you remind me of a story, starts Lincoln. Another one of his roguish yarns. A bawdy type of chatter, a rail-splitting, chain-gang story, a perverse parable. Lincoln continues: *One afternoon a fellow stopped by the office asking to be appointed minister abroad. Sensing my hesitation, the gentleman came down to a more modest proposal.* The audience snickers. Lincoln adjusts his atrocious hat. *After much of the same to and fro, the man asked to be appointed a tide-waiter.* The crowd crackles to life, even before the punch line. The old bag of wind is like a reoiled machine. There's color in his cheeks, a twinkle in his eye. He strokes his beard and draws out the ending. *Now, let me see.* He smiles, rocks back on his heels. *Where was I?*

"The waiter, the waiter!" yells the crowd.

Oh, yes. When the man discovered he could not have that, he asked me for an old pair of trousers. There's hooting and roaring from all corners of the room. Booth sits on the stage in a droopy pile, playing with his fingers. *My boy,* says Lincoln, *it is best to be humble. Especially when one is illegitimate.*

Booth flushes red. His worst secret revealed by his worst enemy. It is true. Booth is a bastard, the spawn of an unholy entanglement. By rank he is less noble than the bumpkin Lincoln, born in wedlock. Worse, Booth is not really a southerner, as he so often claims. Hailing from Maryland—the gutless, wavering Maryland. Booth feels as if his very face were a fiction, a cloth mask stretched over borrowed bones. He tugs at his hair to make sure it is fixed to his scalp, and it plucks out in lovely curls. He gasps. He goes to scream but his teeth fall out of their sockets, long and narrow with ghastly pointed roots. He wakes with a furious heart.

LINCOLN

Lincoln's story is one perhaps best told by others, the ones left behind. Those things and people in Lincoln's employment during his final days. What remains is a curious testimony. Loosely stitched and, of course, unfinished.

His picture: Of the hundreds of images taken of Lincoln, one photograph is without question the most striking. One of a series of formal shots, taken the morning after Lee's surrender. He is seated in an ornate chair, its four legs formed from a series of polished wooden bulges, that in twos resemble the curves of a woman's body. His legs extend forward toward the camera, long and crooked like the branches of a thin tree. His polished dress shoes could hold a half-gallon of milk apiece, and a little more. He rests his arms uncomfortably in his lap, thumb and forefinger of each hand pinched as if he were measuring salt or conducting music. He wears a wrinkled, silk-collared jacket, a white dress shirt that is loose in the chest, and a lopsided bow tie. His hair, reasonably smoothed, is recently thinned. His beard—grown as a disguise while he took the railroad to Washington City for his first inauguration—has, in four years' time, grown thick and then thin again, patchy in the cheek. Perhaps Lincoln loses his hair from sheer exhaustion. The follicles quit their grip on the strands.

Lincoln eats a bird's diet and rarely sleeps. At times it seems impossible that he is alive. Lines mark his face cruelly—long and deep. His flesh is loose on the bone, and his eyes have ceased to hold color. They are now like the skin settled over warm milk. Translucent, tenuously draped over a weak surface, barely holding shape. On this day of victory he looks like someone who is disappointed with death. He looks like someone who has been kept waiting a long while.

His Doorman: The doorman is one of four guards hired to protect the President during the last months of his life. The guards are chosen more for their size than know-how. There is no reason to trust any of them to act well in a bad situation.

One spring evening, well past midnight, one of the doorkeepers hears a nearby, double-barreled gunshot. He wrings his hands under the dim light of the White House's front entrance. Who else but the President would draw fire in the darkest hour of morning? The doorkeeper looks up and down the avenue, searching for light in the shuttered windows of neighboring hotels. All is dark. There is no moon. Soon the doorman perceives the gathering, crooked rumble of hooves over cobblestone. He peers down the avenue and recognizes the President, dwarfing his full-grown horse. Lincoln is bareheaded and without a jacket. His white shirt flaps in the wind. He struggles with the reins, half standing in the saddle and tugging back at the horse's long neck. Lincoln jolts to a halt and dismounts, breathing heavy.

"Riding alone again, sir?" says the doorman.

"I can't seem to get to sleep." Lincoln hands over the reins and smoothes the horse's mane.

"What happened to your hat?" The President is never outdoors without his trademark stovepipe.

Lincoln touches his hair absently. "I must have lost it." He nods good night and shuffles inside, stooped. He is thin and weary looking, his hair blustered into haphazard curls.

The doorman ties the horse at the front gate and leaves his post. He is not one for standing still, even under orders. He treks up the road, heels clicking on the stone. He walks in the middle of the street, head down. The square stones are wet with spring, caked with mud, swelled and upturned in places where they've burst with cold. On instinct the doorkeeper turns down a narrow alley between two boarding houses. The muddy pass is lined with garbage. A loose rooster pokes around in the dirt, clucking idly, pecking at various smelly heaps. It is not uncommon for fowl to roam the streets, feeding themselves from discarded scraps. What is peculiar about this rooster is its shape, its walk. The doorkeeper watches its silhouette for some time. The rooster seems to struggle under the weight of its own wattle, tipping forward and losing its footing. The doorkeeper inches closer. In better light he sees that the rooster beaks the President's hat, which dangles and dips in the mud. He stalks forward, crouching, hands outstretched. The rooster squawks and flaps its wings, attempts flight. But the stovepipe is too much to bear. The doorman stomps his feet and manages a low growl. The bird releases the hat with what appears to be a certain amount of grief, as if it were abandoning the body of a favorite child. The doorman scoops the collapsed hat and examines it in the dark. It is mud-covered, the black silk patched with stains, the brim trampled and bent. The top is tilted like a crumbling chimney.

Then he confirms his worst fear: The crown of the hat is pierced with a fat hole, the wound of serious ammunition. This marks the third known attempt on Lincoln's life, the closest shot yet. A bullet whisked through the hat's narrow cylinder, inches from Lincoln's head. Still, until the very night of his death, Lincoln continues to ride alone at night, Paul Revere-ing around, announcing his sorrow at every door.

After Lincoln's death, the doorman cannot help himself. He tells the story to anyone who will listen. Each time it is different. Each time his own role improves. Sometimes there is no rooster, and the doorman finds the hat in a driveway. Sometimes the doorman is shot at by rebels trying to finish the job. It is always the same with the hat, though. Pierced through the crown. A miss so narrow and terrifying it defies explanation, no matter how many times he tries, no matter how fantastic the circumstances.

The doorkeeper never forgives himself. He rubs his fingers together absently, obsessively, for the rest of his life, imagining the silk hat against his skin, its thin, crumpled frame, its black band of mourning. He recalls the fabric torn in a rough circle, how the bullet left a star-shaped scar.

His Chair: Lincoln is shot in a rocking chair. John Ford, the owner of the theater, brings the chair from his own residence when the President plans to be in attendance. Surely the President esteems the chair's construction, the ease it allows his legs. Or maybe he simply admires its beauty. It is a sleigh built for one. Cushioned in a rich red fabric, puckered with covered buttons, swollen at the neck with extra padding. The slender arms are carved from a dark wood. They run straight for the length of an average arm, then dip toward the floor and curl under themselves. The four legs are short and fat, perched on long, thin rockers. Today the chair would be placed in a nursery. It is small and delicate enough to raise suspicion. How could a man of any size—and a President at that—favor such a dainty throne? The top of the chair is marked with a biscuit-sized stain, seeped into the upholstery, thought by some to be Lincoln's blood. In fact it is the mark of a popular gentleman's hair pomade. In terms of evidence, indications of the President's brief and tragic patronage, the chair offers nothing. No print, no stain.

From Booth's vantage, the chair poses a particular problem. High backed, it obscures most of Lincoln's head, leaving a narrow, crescent-shaped target. Booth slows his breathing and pulls a brass-handled gun from his vest. He aims deliberately, both arms extended, head cocked. On stage, the play continues with its comic twists. Booth's shot is not heard over the crowd's laughter. When a frenzied man leaps to the stage waving his pistol, the crowd believes it is part of the script. Some clap and chuckle, drowning out Booth's dramatic parting soliloquy: *Sic semper tyrannis!*

Meanwhile the rocking chair thrusts forward and washes back, allowing Lincoln's body to ease into the blow. Perhaps it spares him a certain amount of pain. Doctors stretch him across the floor, find the wound, and work a clot from the back of his head, just above the left ear. Someone provides brandy. Someone parts his lips and eases in the fluid. False blood, false hope. Someone holds his hand the nine hours it takes him to die.

Later, someone washes the blood from his hair, loosens the dried stain with water, sets it running again. Later, someone places silver coins over his swollen eyes to weigh down the lids. And later, the chair retires to an ill-frequented museum. It creaks and sighs whenever it is cleaned.

BOSTON CORBETT

His picture: Not an unattractive man. His long hair is parted down the center and pulled together at the nape of the neck. He wears ill-fitted Union blues, a fat stripe running along the vertical seam of his loose trousers. He sits at a round table reading an enormous Bible. He is clean shaven. His boots are knee-high, made of black leather, and have probably trampled across acres of blood-soaked ground.

Before Boston Corbett shot John Wilkes Booth at close range with a Colt revolver, he was a sergeant in the Union Army, and before that, a hatter in Boston, Massachusetts. One of twenty-six men hired to pursue Lincoln's killers, Corbett did not shoot Booth under orders, in self-defense, or any other set of condoned circumstances save this: God told him to. The mandate from Secretary of War Stanton was to round up Booth alive and squealing. What good was a public hanging of the conspirators without their gallant leader, the most famous actor in Washington City? At the very least, Booth would provide an afternoon's entertainment, his final speech choked out as his trim legs kicked uselessly over the platform. Instead, Stanton has to settle for a dead fugitive, shot in the neck by a mad hatter. As Secretary of War one learns to take what one can get.

It seems that Corbett was always waiting for this to happen— that he had spent his life in preparation for this one act, this favor to God. Even as he shaped hats in Boston he was practicing the gestures of precision, studying the relationship between his methodical labor and its eventual divine purpose. Just as Jesus spent a certain amount of time learning carpentry, Corbett apprenticed himself in a tidy shop, fixing practical hats to warm his neighbors' heads.

Hats are made by hand then, meticulously. It is rare for a gentleman to walk the streets with an uncovered head. Every respectable man owns at least two, one for dress and a second for weather. It is considered good form to touch the brim of one's hat upon passing an acquaintance, to remove the hat completely when bowing to a lady. In Washington City, the fancy top hat is in style. A black collapsible wool-felt blend with a ribbon trim. The streets are teeming with them. A taller-than-average person can watch the hats from above, clogging the streets with black and brown and gray, bobbing to and fro like shifting silt, like fish bellying around on a lake's surface. Corbett is familiar with the President's unusual choice in head wear. The lonely, poor-selling stovepipe. Why an overly tall man wishes to accentuate the problem is his own business. Corbett makes a few hats on the chance that locals will want to imitate the presidential fashion. He sells one to a traveling merchant, and the others sit on a shelf for most of Lincoln's administration.

In this part of the country the practical fur hat is still in style. Corbett works late in the shop washing the bloodied pelts of beavers and muskrats. He wets the fur in a basin of water, then soaps vigorously. The fur makes a munching noise against itself. Corbett runs the soap up his own arm, his hairless skin pink with foamed blood. When the pelt dries he applies mercury to the separate the skin and fur. He rubs it into the roots with his fingers, and the poison seeps through his skin. He takes a moment to admire the cool liquid, how it skates across his palm and divides into an arrangement of spheres, like planets and their moons, a whole universe in silver reflecting the warm pink of his palm. He thinks of God's hand and his place in it. A small mirror.

The hair pulls from the skin and Corbett steams it onto sections of felt. His fingers are silver-tipped. When he licks them after a meal he sucks on the poisonous traces. It tastes like suffering. There are flecks of mercury in his blood, running slick through the veins like silver bullets, up to the brain. The mercury chimes in his head, God's voice. Corbett's hats become something of a legend in town. So precisely detailed, so finely stitched, so comforting and necessary. Tucked in the store window, such small and attractive wonders.

One summer Corbett works for a few weeks without hearing from God. His hats turn out mediocre, and he begins to worry that he has sinned in some way. He examines himself with unflinching scrutiny before settling on a minor transgression. Lately his thoughts have wandered some. He has begun making ladies' hats, harmless enough. But in the process he has on occasion imagined himself unfastening a lady's bonnet, soaping a woman's hair right there in the shop, in his basin. He has even looked wantingly at the prostitutes across the street in their feathered caps.

Corbett crosses the dark room to examine an unfinished bonnet, sprawled across a workbench like a spider. The bonnet is light in his hands, made of a fine off-white muslin, lace-edged with mother of pearl buttons under the chin. He strokes the fabric with his fat, red thumb. He circles the chin's button with a finger. *Women and their articles,* he thinks, and rips the button loose. It pops on the floor like a weak gunshot. The room seems to shrivel. Its blue walls slant inward and the floor pushes up. It is always this way when Corbett thinks of women—their stifling and irresistible bodies. His breath comes quick, and suddenly the fumes clog his breathing. There is only one solution.

Corbett castrates himself with a pair of scissors to avoid the temptation of women. Only one of the sacrifices a true man of God must be willing to make. For it is better for a man not to marry, lest he be distracted from the Lord's work. Corbett sharpens the blades on a rod to make the music of a ritual. Afterward, he wraps himself in the same manner used to diaper Jesus on the cross.

Corbett then eats a generous dinner and makes conversation at the table. He uses the right fork at the right time and remembers his prayers. He retires casually and takes a short stroll around the neighborhood before deciding to visit the hospital.

He is now a passionless man, unsuited for war. But he joins the Union Army, and re-enlists several times to preserve the sanctity of the whole. And now, to ensure the final peace, he is sent after Booth to end it all. In his own estimation, Corbett serves as the final blow in the Civil War.

On April 26, 1865, Corbett and his company track Booth to a tobacco farm in Northern Virginia. They have been twelve days on the hunt. The Virginia spring is cold, the pale grass still scattered loose over the frozen earth, crunching under their boots. It is a lot like war. The men keep low as they file through rows of planted greens and circle a large barn, weapons poised.

The barn is a limp wooden structure, warped in places and leaning to one side. Inside, Booth and his toady, David Herold, make assessments. A dozen Blues at least, maybe two. Closing in on them. The commander orders an immediate surrender and Herold, tired from days of scavenging, knows it is over. He steps from the barn, arms raised. Booth remains, waiting for the soldiers to approach. He picks up an old scythe from the corner of the barn and leaps around, slicing through the air. He holds it like a woman and takes a final spin around the barn. So little room for Booth's beloved gymnastics. The floor of the barn is littered with scraps of old tobacco. One of Booth's favorite smells, warm and genteel. The fumes engulf him. The soldiers have lit the barn on fire, and the flames leap from the ground high and fat, smoking furiously. The tobacco curls under the heat, mulching the floor. There is a crackled roaring, and the air goes soft, rising in waves. Booth decides to make a run for it, and he stands for a moment, gets into character.

Outside, Corbett inches closer to the barn, crouching under the heat. Squinting, struggling for breath. It is something of a miracle that a man in this situation gets off a fatal round. Through a crack in the barn, two warped boards separated with a six-inch gap. Corbett raises the revolver. He aims through the traces of his own breath.

The bullet lodges in Booth's neck, severing the spinal cord. While the shot still sounds in the air, while the powder from Corbett's revolver lingers over the earth, several men race into the barn and drag Booth from the flames. One of the men swipes Booth's hat with a mind to sell it to the highest bidder. The other men take turns guarding the body. Booth remains conscious for a few hours but says little. It is not until his final moments that Booth asks the soldiers to hold up his paralyzed hands before his face, so he can admire them. The soldiers take turns puppeteering. Booth stares into his palms and utters the word *useless* on his next to last breath. These faces peering over him. He flutters his eyelids and practices his most disdainful expression. An act? It is hard even for Booth to say.

FORECAST

Boston Corbett is excused of all criminal charges in the shooting of John Wilkes Booth. He moves to Kansas, where he is less of a celebrity, and takes a job as doorkeeper for the State House of Represent-atives in Concordia. He tips his hat to the representatives on their way in and out of session. He stands with his hands clasped behind his back and guards the door while men of good faith discuss earthly situations. Corbett imagines God's house to look a little like this, a single room where one must answer to his sins, where one is con-sidered for approval or disapproval. Where one is discussed in a rea-sonable manner and occasionally fought over, good against evil un-til someone wins out. Corbett keeps his post without incident until one afternoon when he overhears two representatives mocking the ceremonial opening prayer. He pulls a derringer from his pocket and waves it around the room. He is seized and institutionalized be-fore getting off a shot. Upon his release he tells a friend that he is headed for Mexico, and is never heard from again. Possibly he makes it all the way south, where he is recognized by no one. Where the hats are fat and wide and simple, made of cheerful straw. Possi-bly he dies happy.

Perhaps Booth suffers the worst fate of all. He simply dies. He leaves a legacy of a name and little more. The occasional footnote, the odd wax statue in roadside museums. Historically, Booth is cast as the rogue and Lincoln the gentleman. If anything, Booth only heightens Lincoln's fame.

Lincoln is the first President to be depicted on American cur-rency. A bill and a coin, both in threat of extinction. Given the pop-ularity of the one and the ten, who needs a five? Pennies are kept in children's banks, out of circulation. There is talk of abandoning the cent, rounding everything to the nearest nickel. But no one can bring himself to do it. The whole system breaks down, falls apart in the absence of its smallest denomination.

The money artists are flattering. Lincoln's features are softened on the currency, his hair brushed in place. The penny's face shows Lincoln in profile with a regular nose and a dainty ear. We have our way with him. His image becomes something else, someone else, minted a thousand times over, practically worthless.

Lincoln's truest image is the least known. Look close at the tail side of a new penny. Between the two middle columns of the Lincoln Memorial you can make out a miniature seated figure. It is barely perceptible when new, nothing more than a scratch, and the first thing to rub off with time. Scraped against the cashier's drawer and moistened with sweaty fingers. He is always sitting far off, waiting to escape, to slip between our fingers, to ride off unaccompanied and catch his death. Now it is hardly worth the trouble to fetch a penny off the ground.

Going Out of Business Forever

Other kids watch for South Dakota license plates, wheels without hubcaps, blown headlights. In my father's car we scout for men in black sedans who speak into their sleeves. Men wearing dark, gold-rimmed glasses and somber fedoras. We're on the lookout for cars with plenty of trunk space. Beware of the fat cigar, the upturned collar on a trench coat.

Today our father is charged with a handful of errands. Our mother asked him to get out of the apartment and give her some goddamned peace and quiet. Take the twins to the dentist. Pick up a turkey, cat food, a Christmas tree. Fill the tank with gas. Five things, Jeff, not too much to ask. Take your coat and come right back. Don't go off on another one of your world tours.

It's the 'eighties, decade of high-flying optimism, and our family is determined to fight off decay. To drape itself in the gewgaws of normality. Two kids and a cat, tinsel on the tree. Regular trips to the dentist, our teeth polished, the holes plugged with silver.

Our father is a reporter with the *Worcester Telegram.* His picture in the newspaper bears an unfortunate resemblance to Burt Reynolds. People are always writing in about it, and so he's trying

51

to grow a beard to disguise the likeness. Our mother works at Friendly's restaurant. She treats us like her sisters, which means that we get to try on her heels and watch *Dynasty*, but which also means that we cook for ourselves. My twin sister, Fiona, already has her eye on the White House. She makes the best grades in school and practices giving orders at home. She keeps an autographed picture of Ronald Reagan taped inside the bedroom closet, behind our clothes, where our father can't see it. Occasionally she sends the President handfuls of jellybeans in business envelopes. My father says when I grow up I can be Fiona's decoy, that she'll need a good one. Which I am, her exact twin, born second for just such a purpose.

Today, though, we will be made appreciably different. Fiona has a cavity in an upper right molar, and mine is lower left.

Our father parks the car at his choice of meters, cuts the engine. "Ladies," he says. "A little bit of fatherly advice."

Fiona rolls her eyes, sulks at the side-view. She is slumped so dramatically in the front seat she might be dead.

"Do *not* take the shot," our father says. "Needle long as your arm. He flexes his jaw, shows five molars jacketed in silver, like a general's stars. "Never a shot for me," he gloats. He describes the tremendous swelling provoked by novocaine, the tendency to bite through one's tongue.

Which reminds him, by the way, of how pocketless Russians once carried coins in their mouths. They had to endure the tang of suffering. And they paid for goods by fishing under their tongues for rubles, spreading disease. But then Peter the Great comes along with his revolutionary change purse. "Try it," he says. "*Ruble*. What a word." This is our father's pastime, this trivia, this history of strife.

All the time he is talking, his glasses catch the light reflected by the snow, which is everywhere. He is a man with glasses with nothing behind them, as in cartoons.

"What a parking space," he says. Although the street is empty. Is always empty, the dentist being the last surviving business on the block. I press a quarter into the meter, and the red needle hacks forward, buys time. A lousy pole, its head swollen with change.

The dentist's office is a building in the shape of a trapezoid, brick on three sides, the fourth a sheet of thick glass, dimpled and green, angled toward the sidewalk. Through which the people inside look muted and hopeless, as though trapped under water.

The dentist is a man with a morbid flair for decorating. There are model human skulls placed about the waiting room, their long yellow teeth supposed to scare us into flossing. The carpet is stiff and orange, spotted with metal folding chairs. We sit. Our father takes up with a cardboard children's book. Fiona examines her fingernails. She takes every opportunity to groom. Smoothing her eyebrows, pressing her long eyelashes between fingers, to curl them. She assesses the health of her hair. Waist-length and nearly black, our hair is so thick it seems inappropriate on twelve-year-old girls. It is our most notable feature by far. Our faces are long and thin, the miserly faces of librarians and grandfather clocks. And so Fiona sits and practices positioning her jaw in ways that give her face a softer line.

The usual turquoise chair, tools hanging from jointed metal sticks. The dentist plinks around, making preparations.

"No shot," I tell him. "I don't want a shot."

The dentist tugs at the high collar of his smock with a crooked finger. "I would advise," he says, "a shot. Please." He continues, intensely slow, as if speaking to a toddler. He describes the tooth's root as a kind of miniature dragon, who breathes fire whenever disturbed. The dentist mimes horror, claws at the air. "That will be you," he says, in a breathy Hitchcock drawl. "Trust me." He lowers his set of square glasses, which are strapped to his forehead. His eyes are grossly magnified, wet and beseeching.

"No shot."

The dentist pokes at a sliver of metal in its pleated paper cup. Frowns. Quick, a lump of cotton wadded against the cheek. And the drill.

Our father has been an active Communist ever since we were born, but in recent months he's quit the party and downgraded to a home-based, nonspecific loathing of the human race. Now that he's around, the apartment seems overcrowded. At dinner, someone has to squeeze between the kitchen table and the wall. Fiona and I are still in the process of adjusting to his habits. He yells at the television. Every newscaster is a bastard. He tends to rearrange the dishwasher after you've loaded it. He suddenly cares about the quality of our bed making, the alphabetical arrangement of books in their case. He lets the phone ring unanswered. And the only time he ever places a call is when he wishes to inform various mail-order solicitors of his recent death. "You must stop sending brochures to this address," he always says. "Not that it's any of your business, but he was run over by a Pinto. Yes," he says. "Very unfortunate."

It wasn't so long ago that our father had larger concerns. Most of his free time was devoted to an underground newsletter called the *Working Man's Bugle*, which he wrote for under an assumed name, Clyde Snavely. Clyde Snavely spent his evenings with the *Bugle* staff, at various covert meetings, until he published a suggestive article about Worcester's Cavanaugh family. The Cavanaughs own a car dealership and two restaurants. They are holders of a vast fortune of unknown origin, friends of the police and the President. Our father cringes at their every success.

Since publishing the article, our father imagines himself to be in grave danger. He secretly believes that every trip to the grocery may be his last. So he drives across town for a gallon of milk, takes a different route to work each morning. He prefers back doors, dentists of ill repute.

The hygienist steers me back to the waiting room, and my father jumps up to retrieve me, a dead goose from the mouth of a clever hound. "Hey, buddy," he says. He picks up a basket of lollipops from the receptionist's desk, their small colorful heads the size of quarters. "Have a pop. How'd it go?" And so begins a fit of guilty solicitation that will last an hour.

The logical choice would be to head for home, where there's a grocery full of turkeys right behind our apartment, its lot crammed with Christmas trees. And a nearby gas station of the type our father prefers, locally owned by a man named Lenny. But we're miles from home. Our father says it's better to keep driving until we locate the absolute lowest price on a gallon of gas. Several months ago, Clyde Snavely had predicted a drastic rise in oil prices in an unpopular column titled "What You Don't Know About J. R. Ewing."

"Would you just pick one and get it over with," says Fiona. She's in the front seat, combing her hair.

"Yes, dear," he says.

"I don't know what the big deal is," she says, attacking a snarl. "If you'd just gone to the first one we'd be home by now."

Our father passes up another string of gas stations. "Did I mention you girls should never, never agree to a credit card?" he says, looking into the rearview. Lately he's been imparting fatherly knowledge. In the event of his sudden disappearance, we'll at least know a thing or two about life. "They put your name in this computer. And then they control you." He taps on the horn. He tends to do this when he makes an important point, which is unfortunate, since it draws attention. "And another thing," he says. "When you're buying eggs, you should always consider brown. Support the small farmer. When you're shopping in Tuscaloosa, or Green Bay, or Transylvania, or wherever you each should roam, never let anyone tell you that brown eggs are inferior to white."

"When are we going to the store?" says Fiona.

"Right," says our father. "Coming, coming. Any minute now."

"You're not supposed to be driving around all day."

"Yes, dear, quite right." More and more, our father treats Fiona like a second wife. He does whatever she says. He allows her to yank him from daydreams.

"And slow down, Mom said."

It's true that we're flying. Our father believes in the left lane, the hydroplane. That way, no hired gun can keep up.

"You should relax, Clyde," Fiona says. "Nobody reads the *Working Man's Bugle* anyway."

When we finally pull up to the grocery, I'm still thinking about Tuscaloosa, Green Bay, Transylvania. I'm thinking about the possibility of moving. I'm wondering what's keeping us here.

Understand that we live in Worcester, Massachusetts, where nothing good ever happens. People here resist progress. The last technological advance we fully embraced was the windbreaker jacket. We're the world capital of obsolete inventions. Honorary home of the telegraph, the steamboat, the 8-track. The inside of every storefront window is glazed with circles of soap. We're all going out of business forever.

As a city we are notable in tour guides for only three reasons. First: the Higgins Armory Museum, a miniature castle with false turrets, which houses the largest collection of armor in the world. The tour is self-guided. You wander through the dark, torch-lit halls. Every so often you encounter an empty, dimpled suit of armor standing guard. There's the occasional display of medieval weaponry encased in glass. A studded club, a forty-pound sword, a board with a nail in it. There's a chain mail suit, its links glistening like the gills of an exotic fish, the last of its species, trapped in an aquarium. It's the only field trip our school is willing to pay for. I've been five times.

Second: Union Station, former command center of the Worcester-Providence railroad, now a condemned building. Its once-white face is sooty with exhaust, like a marshmallow left too long over a flame. The domed roof hunches over its four columns, and seems in perpetual danger of collapse. Even so, we are flattered when a team of clipboard-wielding scholars says Union is of extreme architectural importance, the last standing example of a particular type of foyer. They try and fail to raise funds for renovation. And so Union remains condemned, a popular murder site. Two months earlier, Scotty Truman, our downstairs neighbor who was in line for a baseball scholarship to UMass, and who Fiona used to be in love with, was shoved off the roof of the station by an unknown party. Scotty used to work at Cavanaugh's Restaurant. His accident was one of several unexplained phenomena that provoked Clyde Snavely's interest. People say Scotty was lucky to survive, but I'm not sure. Though he's seventeen, he's now back in the fourth grade.

Third: One thing to be proud of, we know our place. Worcester is home to the world's first diner. The quick, uncomplicated meal. Then and now a measure of convenience for the weary traveler who is undoubtedly headed elsewhere. Even those who live here prefer the sense of the temporary. We keep our jackets on at church and eat dinner standing. The car is always running in the drive.

We've succeeded in buying a twelve-pound turkey and a six-foot tree without incident. When we pull up to the house Scotty Truman is standing in the front yard up to his ankles in snow, swinging an aluminum bat at imaginary pitches. Baseball is one of the things that survived the accident. He's forgotten long division, but his swing is as swift and level as a pro's. He squints off in the distance, waggling the bat below his hips. Then he rears back and swings. We all imagine the ball soaring across the street, over the roof of the Monsieur Donut Shop, and we follow an imaginary arc. Scotty trots a diamond through the snow and, surprise, he's next at bat. Every swing is a home run.

You'd mistake Scotty for a normal adult except he's dressed like a scarecrow, in loose overalls and a red flannel shirt. He wears a pair of yellow rubber boots. His blond hair is shaved down to a shadow, something he never would have allowed before. Scotty's mother, Marsha, is primarily concerned with matters of convenience. He'll wear pants with elastic waistbands and pull-on shoes the rest of his life. Marsha is our landlady, who lives on the first two floors, who is our mother's only friend. Marsha often mourns the unfairness of a second round of mothering, having come so close to freedom.

"Hi there, sport," our father says, untying the rope from the half-closed trunk.

"Hi," Scotty yells.

"How about coming up tonight? You want to help decorate this tree?"

Scotty is so excited he doesn't know what to say. He looks at Fiona and me for a few seconds, all smiles, before dropping the bat and running inside. "Oh, boy; oh, boy; oh, boy," he says, giggling all the way up the stairs. You can hear everything that happens in our house from any point in the yard.

"You girls should make an effort to say something," we're told. "Don't just stand there like mimes. Nobody likes a mime."

Fiona mimes like she's crying, her mouth open, rubbing her eyes with fists. "Gimme a break," she says. He doesn't hear her. He's leaning into the trunk trying to exhume the Christmas tree. Every year he buys a tree he can't handle.

Fiona heads inside. She leaves small, determined prints in the snow. I try to place my feet exactly in her trail. I walk past Scotty's bat, which is sunk in the snow, which means he probably won't be able to find it later. I take it up and try a few swings. It's heavier than I thought. I pull a muscle in my arm and decide to leave the bat on the porch.

My father's got the tree by its trunk. I hold the door open while they squeeze through. The spruce is so fat it takes up the whole width of the stairwell, rustling over every step. "Son of a bitch," he says, gasping at the first landing. He sets down the tree and wipes his forehead with his sleeve. He combs his moustache with two fingers, catching his breath. Watching him rest on the landing is like watching a stage actor fuss in the wings. He is settling into the tree ritual. It's the only time he ever swears.

He won't look me in the eye. I decide to go out and shut the trunk of the car, which is open and collecting snow. I find the turkey resting in the belly of the spare tire, covered in green needles. It's mine to carry.

Our mother has gone back to bed, so our father fights with the spruce in a hushed growl. They go the distance, leaning against each other, our father breathing heavy, trying to keep the tree on its feet, trying to force it into its corner in a sand-filled bucket. The tree won't stand. Every time it looks straight, it slumps over, spraying the carpet with sand. Our father son-of-a-bitches his way through the first few rounds in a controlled voice. Fiona and I play Old Maid at the kitchen table, snickering at his misfortune.

Finally our mother emerges from her bedroom and shuffles down the hall in her slippers. She loves to drag her feet.

"Don't tell me you did it again," she says, zipping up her royal-purple housecoat.

"I did," he answers, from somewhere behind the tree.

"Girls, I was counting on you." She shakes her head at us.

"I tried to stop him," says Fiona. "He wouldn't listen."

"You're your own worst enemy," she tells him. "What's wrong with a normal-size tree?"

"This was the better value." He makes a few pathetic straining noises. Our mother sighs. She informs us that there's a Doris Day movie on Channel 38 about to start in her room, and that we should leave our father alone so he can swear.

"You're an angel of mercy," he tells her. They kiss. They still do that sometimes.

"I'm staying in my pajamas all day," she announces. "Isn't it exciting?" It's her first day off work in weeks. Her black-and-white checked waitress dress hangs from the closet door. It still holds the shape of her body. There are two slight dents where the fabric is too tight around her breasts. Today we see her long red hair out of its usual bun. Times like these she is still girlish, the kind of woman you'd expect to see advertising milk.

After an hour our father has graduated to son-of-a-bitch-of-a-bastards, shouted at the top of his lungs. The three girls, as our mother likes to say, are marooned on her queen-size bed, waiting out the storm. It's a lot like camp. Our mother confides a few things while braiding our hair, like any good counselor. She warns us that being married to a Communist isn't easy. Your husband at a certain point begins to find your suffering endearing. He finds you attractive at odd, frugal moments, like when you're rinsing out a plastic sandwich bag to use again, or when you're wiping the kitchen table with a rag. Soon you begin to suspect he loves you best when you act in ways that remind him of his mother. Nothing would make him happier than to see you wielding a scythe in the backyard, or carrying two pails of water dangling from a yoke. If only you could yodel.

By the way, it is worth noting that a Communist is still better than no husband at all. Just ask Doris Day.

In return, we offer our mother a view of our teeth, mouths open like baby birds clamoring for food. "Dad calls this the tang of suffering," Fiona says. "Not featured in most movies." We tell her the story of the drilling, the refused needle. Clearly a mistake. This changes our mother back to an adult. She's ready to sulk, to smoke a long chain of cigarettes. To ignore our father for several days.

When I venture to the kitchen during a commercial, the tree's down again and he's kicking it across the carpet. "You goddamn bastard," he yells. The tree sways, slightly bemused. He drags the tree into the kitchen and lifts it onto the table.

"Do me a favor there, Francie," he says. "Look under the sink and find the saw."

I do.

"Do you know what this is?" he says to me, taking the saw by the blade. He indicates the tree's trunk. It's the usual brown, but it bulges in places like a can infested with botulism. "This is a split stem. It's like two goddamn trees grown into one." He's right. One side of the tree is a bright blue-green, and the other side is paler. "It's uneven," he says. "Any way I stand this it'll fall, see?" He goes to work sawing at the trunk. He uses exaggerated movements—

some knee bending, some teeth gritting. He's a hammy magician sawing through his assistant.

"Do you see what I'm trying to do here?" he says.

"Not really."

"I have to make it even. I've got to trim down one half to save the other." He cuts through the stem and starts slicing away at the bottom branches. It's like the time when Fiona tried to trim her own bangs. She kept evening up until there was just a short spike left. I stay long enough to realize that both halves are useless. It'll be a while before he can bring himself to give up.

We hear the door slam some time before Doris Day gets married, and our father still isn't back when Scotty and his mother, Marsha, show up. Marsha works down the street at Clark University. She's always talking about the way things are done on the college level, even though she dresses almost entirely in animal prints.

"Francine!" she says, like she hasn't seen me in ten years. She grabs me by the shoulders and squashes me into her chest. She's wearing a zebra-print scarf.

"Marsha!" I say, an exact imitation. I'm trying it on for size.

"We're here," she calls. "We're ready to decorate." Scotty is standing by the door, hooking and unhooking the shoulder of his overalls. My mother emerges from the kitchen, where she and Fiona have been spiking eggnog. She points to the tree with a wooden spoon. The tree is split in two, lying in pieces on the kitchen table, like garnish. There's a tangle of branches on the floor. Our father's cat is busy with its first exercise in years, swatting the needles around the linoleum, bewildered by their sleek travel. Green-eyed with a gray coat, the cat is the size of a watermelon, fattened on table food and backyard rodents.

"Look what Jeff did," she says.

"Would you look at that." Marsha wiggles into the kitchen and gives the branches a few pokes with her purple satin shoe. She and my mother start giggling. They often share a laugh at my father's expense. They'll drink eggnog for the rest of the night and discuss Marsha's recent dates. Scotty stands just outside the kitchen, hands in his pockets, peeking at the tree.

"Mom?" he says. "When are we gonna decorate?"

"You know, it's too bad," Marsha says to us, in a tortured whisper. "He was really looking forward to this. It's hard for him to understand not everything works out."

"You know what?" our mother says. She crosses the room and puts her arm around Scotty. "How'd you like to decorate the windows?" she leads him into the living room. "How about we put some lights here?" She traces the window frame with her finger. By day we have a good view of the loading garage at the back of the Big G market. But now it's so dark you can't see past the glass, past our mother's and Scotty's yellow reflections. He's taller by a head. Our mother enjoys the sight of herself in a man's arms.

Scotty gives a short, excited hop. "Where's the lights?"

"Somewhere in the basement," our mother says.

"I know where," says Scotty. "I know."

"He probably does," Marsha says. "He's down there all the time. I hope he hasn't been messing with your stuff. Sometimes I can't get him out of there."

"Can I go? Can I?" He bounces on the balls of his feet.

"Well," says Marsha. "I don't know. It's dark down there." She examines her flamingo-colored fingernails.

"Jeez, Mom."

"Okay, okay." She waves a hand at him.

"Francine," says my mother. "You go with Scotty. Go ahead." She uses the voice reserved for favors.

The stairwell is unheated, and Scotty jumps up and down to keep warm. He stutters down the stairs in his loose boots, and it's a miracle he doesn't fall. "Hey," I say, when we reach the ground floor. "You left your bat outside." It's the first thing I've said to him since the accident.

"Oh, no!" he says. He rushes out the door and scampers around the porch. I follow. We look for a while at the wood underneath our feet. We look at the sky. We look at Scotty's perfect snowman, standing guard on the lawn. Three circles of light and two jointed sticks, positioned to suggest raised arms. It could be defeat, or joy, I can't tell.

You have to devote a certain length of time to looking for something, even when it's certainly gone. "Oh, no," he says. He paces the porch, hands stuffed in the pockets of his silky green Celtics jacket, a get-well present from Cavanaugh's Restaurant. The jacket is many sizes too small. The fit is so tight around his shoulders that the sleeves are starting to unseam from the body. "Oh, no," he says. His eyes fill up. One thing I can't watch is someone crying.

"It's okay," I say. "We'll find it tomorrow. Let's get the lights."

The stairs leading down to the basement are steep and splintery. There's no banister. Scotty has to go down backward, like he's crawling down a ladder, so he can keep his balance. We use the light from the hall. There's a single bulb with a pull chain at the bottom of the stairs, but it's burned out. There's the smell of mildew and fabric softener. There's the smell of things put away for the winter—grass dried on the blades of the lawnmower, the plastic of watering cans. Somewhere in the basement there's a science project I started with a cup of yogurt that was supposed to sit for a week in a dark, damp place, and that I could never bring myself to collect.

We're all the way down the stairs before I notice the smell of someone's cigarette. Scotty lopes off toward a pile of boxes, but I can't move. I'm waiting for my eyes to adjust. And then I'm waiting to see if it's my imagination, or if there really is a shadowed man crouching under the stairwell, a man sitting with his knees pulled in who is rocking ever so slightly, who is holding the slender glimmer of a boy's silver bat tight against his chest, a man whose eyes are wide open with terror, a man who I have not seen before though I have known him all my life.

What the Rabbi Said to the Priest

There were ten beds in the ER, separated by hanging sheets. Doctors and patients were expected to treat these thin sheets like walls. Mark did his best to convince his patients that their embarrassed confessions, their intimate complaints, their profane screams, their meaningless chatter—all of this was confidential. Even in the unlikely event that a patient should be seen or overheard by an acquaintance, he should be assured that there in that cold room— with its white tile floor, its fluorescent lights, its glass jars filled with cotton swabs and tongue depressors, there amidst the glare of stainless steel instruments, the stench of iodine, and the strangeness of polka dot gowns—nothing was easy to recognize. Mark asked his patients not to hold anything back. The emergency room was a place to speak freely about the trouble one had gotten oneself into, to unbosom oneself of even the most scandalous confessions. Patients found themselves telling Mark stories that they had sworn to carry to their graves. Perhaps they were encouraged by Mark's ordinary looks. When patients confided their problems, they felt that they addressed the brown eyes, brown hair, and square jaw of no one in particular.

Mark's first patient that day was an elderly woman whose right arm had been broken for over thirty years. He found her sitting on the bed in her hospital gown, the broken arm folded across her abdomen rather formally, as if she were about to take a bow. She was holding the broken arm in place with her good arm, as she had done for decades. Though she had been waiting for over an hour, the woman sat with her face tilted dreamily, patiently, toward the ceiling. The woman had a nimbus of white hair. She was smiling and rocking ever so slightly, as though she were cradling an imaginary baby.

"Good morning, Mrs. Carmichael," Mark said. He started to extend his hand, to shake, but instead gave the woman an awkward pat on the shoulder.

"How do you do?" the woman said. She spoke slowly, deliberately, with a trace of an accent. It sounded to Mark like the language of royalty.

"Let's see what we have here," Mark said. He took hold of the woman's arm. The muscles of her forearm had atrophied over the years, and so it was disturbingly soft, like a spoiled tomato. The arm had an odd break. The humerus had broken two inches above the elbow, clean in half, and the bone hadn't fused as it healed. So there were two separate and independent sections to the arm, as with jointed wooden toys.

"Does this hurt?" Mark asked, rotating the arm slightly.

"No, doctor," she said.

The lower half of the arm could be moved in any direction. Mark twisted it clockwise, and met with no resistance. It could potentially be wrung like a towel. "No pain at all, here?" Mark asked.

"No, doctor."

"How did you break the arm?" said Mark.

"I fell down a flight of stairs."

"But now, no trouble? No pain at all?"

"I have sensation," Mrs. Carmichael said, "but no pain. At least not in the arm."

"Right," said Mark. "Of course." Mrs. Carmichael had presented with piercing stomach pain. Her arm was another matter, something to which she had adjusted. She had likely endured the curiosity of young doctors, and their superfluous examinations, for decades. Mark let the arm go. Unsupported, it dangled hopelessly.

All morning, while listening to hearts and looking in mouths, Mark couldn't stop thinking about Mrs. Carmichael. There was something about her arm that was worse than the countless deformities that he had seen day in and day out for years. At lunch, Mark read over Mrs. Carmichael's chart. A medical student had noted in the history that the arm had been broken since 1968, but there was no mention of the nature of the accident. More than likely, Mark thought, Mrs. Carmichael had been beaten by her husband. Most of the women who came to the ER with broken bones were carried in by the sorry-hearted men who had nearly killed them.

After lunch, Mark treated a twelve-year-old girl who had cut her finger on a tuna fish can. The girl sat on the hospital bed, swinging her legs. She was tall for her age, and terribly thin. Her brown hair was wildly curly, and it stood almost on end, springing out in all directions. Her hair looked as though it hadn't been brushed in months.

When the girl looked up, Mark saw that she had the triangular face of a cat. She wore large glasses with black plastic frames and lenses so thick that her eyes were spookily magnified—black and roaming, like a shark's. The girl's mother stood next to the hospital bed, her arms folded. The mother's sex was ambiguous. She was morbidly obese, close to three-hundred pounds, and she wore a navy blue sweat suit. She wore her hair in a military crew cut, even shorter than Mark's.

"What do we have here?" Mark said to the girl. "Looks like that fish caught *you.*" The girl was expressionless. Mark waited for her to offer up her finger, but she kept it covered. She was wearing a pink winter coat over her hospital gown, and she pulled its sleeves down over her hands. Mark noticed that the cuffs were gray with grime. "Let's have a look," he said. The girl squirmed, sat on her hands. She looked pleadingly at her mother.

"Sylvie hates needles," said the mother. "Something fierce." Mark was startled. The mother sounded exactly like Elvis.

"No needles," Mark said to the girl. "Let's just look." He touched the girl's pink coat sleeve, and she screamed, the high, piercing scream of a bald eagle.

"Sylvie!" her mother yelled, grabbing her by the elbow. "Jesus hates a crybaby!"

"It's okay, ma'am," Mark said. "Your daughter's just a little scared."

"She's not my daughter," said the woman. "Are you, Miss Skinny Minny?" The girl shook her head, stared into her lap. "Foster child," the woman told Mark. "Since April."

When Mark finally stitched the girl's finger, he saw that her arm—her fragile, scrawny, defenseless arm—was covered in yellow bruises.

Mark had seen hundreds of patients like Sylvie and Mrs. Carmichael—patients who were most likely the victims of troubled households. They always lied about the true nature of their injuries. Earlier in his career, Mark had been enthusiastic about reporting suspected abuse, but now he realized how senseless the whole process was. Wives returned to their husbands, and children to their guardians. It was hopeless. Nothing he did or failed to do would matter. And so Mark was left to brood about his patients. He scowled almost constantly. His forehead was crossed with deep worry lines.

Mark was still thinking about Sylvie and Mrs. Carmichael when he returned home to his wife. He found Ellie standing in front of the bathroom mirror, pulling at her newly short hair. "Look at me," she said. "I'm *hideous*." She didn't turn around to greet Mark, and so they watched each other in the mirror. Ellie made a habit of speaking to him indirectly. A week earlier, while Mark was reading in the bedroom, Ellie had yelled for him to pick up the phone.

She was on the extension in the kitchen. They had spoken for a minute about Mark's schedule, separated by a room. "Why don't you just come in the bedroom?" Mark had asked. "Okay," she said, and hung up. But she stayed put, in the kitchen, hovering over her chocolate soufflé. It had been a magnificent failure.

"You look fine," Mark said now. "Believe me. After what I saw today. You look just fine."

"I suppose that's not saying much."

"Well, that's true," said Mark. "You should have seen this arm. Two arms, really. I can't explain it. The first one, you've never seen anything like it." Mark rubbed his eyes with two tight fists, a habit left over from childhood.

"You're not on call, right?" Ellie asked.

"Right," Mark said. "For the hundredth time."

"Because it's Robby's birthday." Ellie pulled at a curl on the side of her head and tried to tuck it behind her ear. But it was too short and it sprang back, a dark lash.

"I didn't forget Robby's birthday," Mark said. He knew that Ellie was watching him in the mirror, waiting for the slightest expression of distaste. He imagined the evening: dinner at home, a sheet cake bought from the grocery store, decorated with an inane cartoon— a rocket ship, a fire truck—and Robby's tortured attempt at blowing out thirty candles, spraying the cake's surface with saliva. Mark would have to scrape off the frosting. He smiled hopefully.

"Robby wants to go to Madonna's," Ellie said. "He's been hearing about it on the radio."

"Jesus," said Mark.

"What?" Ellie said, turning to him at last. She looked unfamiliar. Her face seemed to have changed since the haircut, smaller, bonier, more fragile than Mark had realized. Her eyes seemed deeper set, more chillingly blue, more distant.

"Nothing. I'm just tired."

"Look alive," Ellie said, and gave Mark a little slap on the cheek. "Robby can tell the difference."

Robby was Ellie's older brother, and her only remaining family. Two months earlier, when Ellie's father had died, she had begged Mark to let Robby move in with them. Mark hadn't made an objection, though the house was small, and his office would have to be converted to a second bedroom. The arrangement was supposed to be temporary, until Robby found a job and an apartment. Ellie had been speaking with some volunteers at the United Way, hoping to place Robby with part-time work. She was hoping to get him a job shelving books at the library, where he could listen to his headphones and work at his own pace. But more likely Robby would end up mopping floors at a grocery store or a fast food restaurant, wearing an ill-fitting polyester uniform.

Now it was Robby's birthday, and he had asked to be taken to the most impractical of places. Madonna's was a nightclub that hosted a cabaret show every Friday night. The show was called Boy Toy, and it featured a dozen award-winning drag queens lip synching and dancing to Madonna songs. Mark knew the club by reputation. Five months ago, the club owners had bought a defunct Catholic church, removed its pews, added a stage, a bar, and a disco ball, started its television and radio advertisement campaign—"Come in and sin!"—and opened its doors. The club had shocked many of the city's residents, who considered it sacrilege. Various religious groups had organized picketing in front of the club, and had kept a nightly vigil for months. They objected to the blinking purple lights that had been attached to the steeple, the blaring music, and the illicit sex that was rumored to take place behind the sacred red curtains in the former confessionals, which, they claimed, had been left intact by the nightclub owners for exactly such a purpose. When news was slow, local reporters stood outside of the club, interviewing patrons and protesters: It was the best of clubs, it was the worst of clubs, it was a club of self-expression, it was a club of blasphemy. Scores of elderly women stood in front of the news cameras holding giant pictures of the Virgin Mary, her head bent in prayer over a swaddled baby. Ellie's only concern with the scandal was the protesters' signs, and their choice to portray Jesus as a baby. "It's just so sick," she said to Mark one night, while they were eating a pizza in front of the television. "How people always insist on bringing out *baby* pictures. No matter how much you accomplish in life."

Mark hated going into the city at night. There was no good reason to be downtown after five o'clock. The streets were poorly lit and eerily vacant, and there were only a handful of buildings with signs of life at late hours—the hospitals, the housing projects, the racetrack, and the dog food factory. Now, of course, there was Madonna's, which seemed to be filling a desperate vacancy in the lives of local young people, who were forced beforehand to amuse themselves outdoors in the parking lots of burger joints and gas stations.

Mark was a nervous driver, and he hated to carry on a conversation while he was concentrating on the road. Normally he and Ellie were content to drive in silence. But since Robby had moved in, there was an awkward void to fill. It seemed to Mark that Ellie had talked more in the weeks since Robby's arrival than she had in the previous two years of their marriage. "So you'll never guess what happened at work," she said, turning in her seat to face Robby. "Today someone ordered a hot chocolate made with half-and-half. That's half *cream*," she said. "Glutton! And then, on top, guess what they wanted on top? Whipped cream!" She laughed, and Robby laughed. He took every cue from her. "Fascinating, right?" Ellie said to Mark. It was an old saw between them. Ellie had been working in a coffee shop for the last two years, instead of finishing her degree. She was sure it embarrassed him. "This is really cutting-edge stuff, here," she said. "I think I might write my thesis on greed and dairy and the human condition." She laughed. Robby laughed.

All the way to the club, Robby leaned forward between Mark and Ellie's seats. "Is that it?" he said, and pointed to a convenience store.

"No," said Ellie. "It's bigger than that. You'll know when you see it."

"That's it," said Robby, pointing to a warehouse.

"Nope," said Ellie. "It's even better. Just wait."

Mark pulled into the hospital parking lot. "We get to park here," he explained to Robby. "This is where I work." But Robby was only interested in the club. His face was pressed to the window. Ellie had just pointed out the purple glow of the club's lights, two blocks away, visible through a maze of abandoned buildings.

Mark was surprised at what people were wearing. There was a long line waiting to enter the club, and it was a streak of zebra-print pants, bikini tops, feather boas, knee-high platform boots, and leather bodices. The season's first flakes of snow were beginning to fall, circling down through the darkness, and these people were dressed for the beach. They shivered in line, clinging to each other, their exposed limbs blue and chickened. Meanwhile the protest-ers were lined on the opposite sidewalk, bundled in downy winter coats. They were puffy blobs of gray, pacing the block like pigeons. It was the fifth month of their protest, and the ranks were wearing thin. They waved their signs wearily, and sang "Ave Maria" ever so softly, slouching through the lyrics, knowing that the noise of the club overpowered them, knowing they wouldn't be heard.

"It's really supposed to storm tonight," Mark said. "Five inches by morning. Enough to make a snowman."

"You hear that, Robby?" Ellie said. "We can make a snowman tomorrow. We can have a snowball fight."

"Yea," said Robby, nonchalant. He stood on his toes, looking to-ward the entrance.

"You *love* snowmen," said Ellie.

"I want to go inside," said Robby. "It's my *birthday*. Tell them it's my birthday." He shoved his hands in the pockets of his Red Sox jacket, which he had worn in all seasons for the past fifteen years. Several of the red letters had unstitched from the jacket over time, and Ellie had sewn them back in place with black thread. The letters were wobbly and uneven, but Mark was fond of Ellie's clumsy stitches. He imagined her teenage hands, attempting the work of a mother.

"Put your hat on," Ellie told Robby, but he pretended not to hear.

"Put it on," she said, and placed her hand on top of his head. He wore a crew cut, so short that his scalp was visible. Ellie was always worried about him catching cold. Robby pulled a knit cap from his pocket and stretched it over his head.

They stood, shivering, looking at the club. It had once been a beautiful stone church, with a high, pitched roof and small stained-glass windows. There were two gigantic front doors, painted red. Mark imagined them being flung open, triumphantly, to introduce a new bride and groom to the world. Mark wasn't religious, but he felt sad at the sight of a failed church. He looked around, suddenly embarrassed. He didn't want to see anyone he knew.

Mark was pleased with his timing. The drag show was scheduled to start just minutes after they bought their tickets. Mark was hoping that the show would last no longer than an hour, and that they would all be home, safe in bed, before too much snow accumulated on the roads. He was looking forward to sleeping late, and spending his first day off in a month under a pile of blankets, his wife in his arms.

The dance stage was at the front of the church, where the altar had once stood. There were card tables and folding chairs arranged at the foot of the stage. Mark and Ellie and Robby brought their drinks to a table and waited for the show to start. Someone was testing the equipment, and a spotlight roamed across the stage, back and forth. The footlights flared up, red and purple and green. Mark knew that when they dimmed the overhead lights, and started with the music and the colored lasers, everyone in the club would overlook the shoddiness of the production, and lose himself in its cheap distraction.

Finally the club went dark. An announcer told the patrons to prepare themselves for the beautiful, the talented, the one-and-only Miss Marvelous. The spotlight wandered around the club for a moment, lighting up the red-and-blue stained-glass windows along the walls. Then the light settled on Miss Marvelous, who was wearing nothing but a green sequined thong, a green feather boa, and a long, blonde wig. The crowd roared. Robby elbowed Mark, flapping his arm like a chicken. "Hubba hubba," he said. It was something he had picked up from a commercial. "She's not wearing a *shirt!*" Miss Marvelous had taken enough hormones to develop small, swollen breasts, and she had glued a green feather over each nipple. She danced haughtily to "Material Girl." Mark was unimpressed. Miss Marvelous lip-synched half-heartedly as she bent over to accept the dollar bills offered up by a line of men that had formed at the foot of the stage. She wiggled a little as she bent for her tips, but it didn't qualify as dancing.

"You know that's a boy, right?" Mark asked Robby. But Robby only wrinkled his forehead.

"Hey, Ellie," Robby said, and whispered fiercely in her ear. "Mark thinks that's a *boy.*" Ellie gave a tremendous laugh, and covered her mouth with both hands, like a schoolgirl. Robby let out his machine-gun laugh, so loud that he drew stares from other tables. They did this often, delighted by something foolish that Mark had done.

"You goof," Ellie said to Mark, and winked.

"I want to go up there," Robby said, all smiles. "Can I?"

Mark said he didn't see why not.

"Here," Ellie said, and offered Robby a handful of bills. They watched him wait his turn in line, waving a dollar bill in the air. Miss Marvelous was not too proud to take it from him. Nor were the dozen other dancers that followed, with names like Queen Most Majesty, Little Miss Thing, Bambi Dearest, and Barbie Knows Best.

A blue-haired man in a pink evening gown was waiting tables, offering four-dollar glasses of warm beer and five-dollar cocktails. The waiter wore a dozen silver hoops in each ear. "Ladies," he said to Mark and Ellie. "Care for a drink?" Mark declined, and the waiter pouted dramatically. "Such a pretty face," he said to Mark. "And not a stitch of makeup." Ellie ordered a whiskey sour. The waiter beamed, and asked for his tip in advance.

"I know that guy," Mark told his wife, when the waiter pranced away in his three-inch heels.

"Great," she said. "I just knew you were seeing another woman."

"Right," said Mark, and snorted. Then he told Ellie that he recognized the waiter from the ER. The waiter was one of hundreds who had been brought in off the street on weekend nights. Every Friday and Saturday there were bar fights, car crashes, drug overdoses. Mark remembered that the blue-haired waiter had been brought in by the police, who had found him in the street, beaten almost to death. It had been sad to see him. He had dressed up for the evening, with high hopes, and had ended up being wheeled into the emergency room on a gurney. Mark remembered that the waiter had been wearing tight leather pants that had to be cut off by the nurses, and an orange silk dress shirt. One shirtsleeve had been torn at the shoulder, and it trailed from the waiter's wrist, by the cuff, like a bright flag. The waiter had been kicked in the ribs so many times that several had broken, piercing a lung.

"So you saved him," Ellie said, and took his hand. "You should be proud."

"It's not that," Mark said, scowled.

"Then what?"

Mark said nothing, only stared at the stage. One of the drag queens was dancing around, dressed as Dorothy from *The Wizard of Oz*. Robby was standing in line, waving a dollar bill. He was barking enthusiastically, along with the other men gathered at the foot of the stage—the *arf-arf-arf* of small, faithful dogs.

"It's not saving someone," Mark said. "It's how they end up like that in the first place." He had to shout over the music.

"Accidents, right?" said Ellie. "Mostly?"

Mark searched, once again, for a way to describe his job to his wife. "My dear," he yelled, "the world is filled with evil. There was this girl today, a foster kid. She was really skinny, and she was wearing this giant coat, which was *dirty*. I mean, it's like they couldn't even afford to wash this girl's clothes." Mark stalled. He could tell that Ellie hadn't understood a word. She was looking up at him, wide-eyed and hopeful. He knew, then, what it was about the girl in the pink coat that had bothered him.

Ellie had worn the same black trench coat almost every day since Mark had met her. It was a man's coat, several sizes too big, in desperate need of repair. The sleeves hung down inches past Ellie's hands. Two of the coat's buttons had fallen off, and there was a hole in each pocket. Ellie thought that the coat suited her.

Ellie had been wearing that coat the night that Mark met her. He had found her outside of a bar, sitting in the parking lot, leaning her head against a light post. It was snowing that night, and Ellie's long, black hair was spotted with white flakes. She sat with her knees pulled into her chest, her coat closed around her legs. She was sitting just a few feet from Mark's car. He walked past her, nodded. She smiled slowly, sadly. Her blue eyes were brilliant, and the rest of the world seemed to lose its color. Mark debated, while he scraped off his windshield, whether he should offer her a ride home.

"So what are you doing sitting here the parking lot?" he said.

"Fresh air," she said. Her voice was faint, childlike. "And the band was terrible." It was true. The band playing that night at the bar was so appalling and so loud that Mark had made excuses to his friends and fled twenty minutes into the set. Mark opened the passenger door of his car and made an awkward gesture. Ellie smiled. She stood and closed her coat tightly around her chest, but she did not move toward the car.

"It's okay," Mark had said. "I'm a medical student."

They drove off, toward campus. At stoplights, Mark tried to make conversation, but Ellie tended to answer his questions with more questions. She wasn't playing by the rules. In the university town in which they lived, every new friendship began with a brief discussion of each person's current studies. In the first five minutes of conversation, everyone spoke of professors and exams and failing dissertations. Ellie only admitted to being a philosophy major with a planned future as an impoverished hermit. Everything she said was vague. Mark couldn't even get her full address.

"Jefferson," she said, referring to a long, thickly settled street that stretched for miles across campus.

"But where?" he asked, "Near the hospital?" Mark was driving down Jefferson now, without knowing where he was headed. Ellie changed the subject. She told him that for years she had had vivid imaginary episodes in which she was kicked in the stomach by field animals. These episodes came to her at odd moments, usually when she was alone, walking to campus, or watching television, or meeting with her professors in their windowless offices, discussing great thinkers. These sensations were so powerful, she said, that sometimes she buckled over and winced. Kicked by a goat, a mule, a camel. "They're lightning fast," she said. "Pow. And then it's over. Have you ever heard of that? Or anything like it? I mean, it's a whole experience. Do you ever get that? Is there a diagnosis for that?"

"No," he said, and slowed the car. He realized at last that Ellie was drunk.

"How about the one where you want to bite people all of a sudden, when they're talking."

"*Bite* them?"

"Or punch them in the face?" She leaned forward and rested her head on the dashboard, then turned to give Mark a sly smile. She was breathing deeply. "Do you ever feel like you've been licked by a thousand cats? Is there any cure for that?" she asked. She blinked her eyes ever so slowly. Once, and again. And then she was asleep. She started breathing through her mouth, her small, chapped mouth. Mark wanted to brush his thumb across her lip. He could, if he wanted to. She had passed out. Mark pulled over and tried to wake her, shaking her by the shoulders. Her head circled, and her neck stretched away from him. It occurred to Mark that this girl might have gotten into a different car with a different man, a man who might not have been able to resist strangling her pale, delicate neck.

Mark wasn't used to having encounters like this. For almost four years of medical school, he had been burrowed in his studies, learning about nothing but disease. All of his conversations were about illness. When he touched people it was with rubber gloves. Mark had gone out that night to the bar with a few friends, celebrating the news of their residency matches. It had been his first social outing in a year. He hadn't expected to meet someone like Ellie, someone so utterly unconcerned with science, someone so impractical, so unabashedly strange. That evening Mark had learned little more about Ellie than he might have learned from her drivers' license. She was a blue-eyed undergraduate with long black hair, a philosophy major interested in Schopenhauer. She had run away from home, taking a scholarship to a school full of rich kids. To her, life was a drag.

Mark had always wanted to know a girl like Ellie. As an undergraduate, he had often wondered about the black-clad philosophy majors who stalked the campus in packs, who smoked cigars, who argued about free will in the back rooms of cafés, and who routinely accused the rest of the student body of stupidity and snobbery. Mark had spent most of his free time conducting experiments in laboratories. He had never played the guitar, or recited poetry, or otherwise wasted his time, which he sometimes deeply regretted.

Mark took Ellie to his house that night, placed her triumphantly on his bed, and covered her with a blanket. But she escaped before dawn, leaving a note by the door. "Remember," she had written, "No rose without a thorn. Many a thorn without a rose." The next day, after his shift at the hospital, Mark walked to the main campus and looked for Ellie. After three hours he finally saw her, crossing a courtyard, headed for the humanities building, slouched under the weight of her backpack. Her long, black hair was in exquisite disarray, flowing behind her along with her billowing black coat. He called to her, started running with his arms raised. He looked ridiculous, he knew, but he couldn't help himself.

Two months later, Ellie was pregnant. Mark had insisted that she marry him. To his great surprise, she agreed. Months later, in a strange town, when their baby struggled for weeks under the warm, pink light of an incubator, and then died, Ellie told Mark that their marriage felt like an elaborate joke with a bad punch line. For days, whenever Mark spoke to her, she answered cryptically.

"So the rabbi says to the priest, 'I thought you were Raquel Welch!'"

"So the rabbi says to the priest, 'What did you expect, a Volkswagen bus'?"

"So the rabbi says to the priest, 'What do I look like, an egg-salad sandwich'?"

Mark had been afraid that Ellie would leave him. She had agreed to the marriage for the baby's sake, and now there was nothing to tie them together. Some mornings, when he woke and found that she was asleep beside him, Mark felt truly surprised.

Ellie was drinking whiskey sours. She had five empty cups stacked in front of her, a squeezed slice of lime rotting in the bottom of each cup. "Easy, there," Mark said to her, when she ordered her sixth. The show dragged on, each dancer worse than the one before. Ellie had grown tired of talking over the music, and she had turned away from Mark. But she talked up a storm with the blue-haired waiter whenever he brought her a drink. They compared the merits of various local thrift stores, hairdressers, political candidates, and restaurants. Finally, Ellie asked the waiter something practical. She wanted directions to the bathroom. "Honey," the waiter told her, "I like you. So I'm gonna let you in on a secret." The waiter leaned conspiratorially over their table and spoke in his unadorned, male voice. "You look like a nice, normal couple. So whatever you do, I'm telling you, don't go in those bathrooms. Okay?" The waiter winked and strutted off, and Ellie's eyes widened. She looked at Mark mischievously. "I wonder," she said, delighted.

"Don't," Mark said. "Don't even think about it."

Ellie sighed, looked toward the stage. "You're such a square," she said, trying for sarcasm, but she was distracted and came off sincere. Her eyes scanned up and down the stage. Then Mark saw a familiar flash of panic seize her face. "Robby," she said, and stood up. She climbed up on her chair and looked around in all directions. "Robby!" she yelled. Mark told her to calm down. Robby would be easy to find—his jacket was one of a kind.

"Shit!" Ellie said, and jumped from her chair. "You go that way." She pushed Mark toward the stage. Then she started off toward the club's entrance, weaving through tables. She was walking unevenly, stumbling drunk.

"Meet me back here," Mark called after her. "Twenty minutes." Ellie waved at him, but didn't look back. Mark caught a glimpse of her delicate, childlike ear, which he wasn't used to seeing. She looked younger and smaller with her short hair. Mark wanted to follow her, to carry her to the car, and take her home. But he knew she would never stand for such treatment.

Mark headed toward the stage. Much of the audience had risen from their chairs and had begun dancing along with the drag queens. Everyone wanted to be part of the show. Mark tried to weave through the crowd, but they were so involved with themselves, their terrible dancing, their terrible conversations, that they wouldn't move to let him pass. "I'm looking for my brother-in-law," he called out. He could hardly hear his own voice over the music. "I just want to find my brother." The club was thick with smoke, and Mark's eyes watered. A strobe light started pulsing, and he could only see people in shocked, white flashes. He saw them gesture with their cigarettes, conducting petty symphonies, smiling, their mouths open, their eyes bulging. They looked clownish, crazed, murderous.

More and more, people disgusted Mark. He was increasingly

overwhelmed with the fatness of his patients, a condition that they could control if they only disciplined themselves. Almost half of the patients he saw in the ER presented with problems related to their weight. There was increased hypertension, heart disease, diabetes, osteoarthritis, gout, and circulatory malfunction. On top of these complications, which fed into each other, it was difficult to perform a decent physical on these patients. Mark had trouble palpating the abdomen, say, if a patient presented with a pain in what he invariably referred to as his "tummy." Sometimes there was so much fat that Mark couldn't hear the patient's heartbeat. A great portion of the country's medical ailments could be entirely eliminated if people watched what they ate, and acted reasonably. But there was no shame, no effort. These fat patients walked around proudly, wearing their pants three sizes too small, the seams riding up the cracks of their preposterous asses. They drove their minivans round and round through the drive-thru windows of fast food restaurants. Meanwhile the cost of health insurance skyrocketed, struggling to keep up with the cost of so many heart attacks.

Mark stood still for a moment, trying to calm the nausea he felt. His job was turning him into something terrible. The only person he could talk to, could touch, was Ellie.

Mark tried to ask people if they had seen Robby. He leaned toward them, yelling in their ears, describing the battered Red Sox jacket, knowing he wouldn't be understood. They shook their heads, they shrugged, they asked him for cigarettes and for dates. On the dance floor someone grabbed Mark's thigh and squeezed. He jerked away, formed a fist, but he couldn't tell who had touched him. For a brief, ecstatic moment, Mark thought he saw Ellie—a tall, slender woman with a sheet of dark hair. He reached for the woman and remembered in that lurch that his wife had cut her hair. Mark saw the blue-haired waiter and hailed him. "Something to drink?" yelled the waiter.

"Have you seen my wife?" Mark asked. The waiter frowned, shook his head, as though he had never seen Mark before in his life.

Mark circled the club, again and again. Twenty minutes had passed since he had last seen Ellie. He knew that he would, at last, have to check the bathroom. It was the first place he should have looked, but he had been cowardly. The bathrooms were located at the end of a long, dark hallway, and Mark could see a small sliver of red light glowing at the edge of each door.

In the women's restroom, Mark saw a girl standing over the trash can, her mouth hanging open. She wore a queasy, seasick expression. Her makeup had run, and her eyes were smeared in black. She was half-dressed, in a miniskirt and halter top. Mark walked past her and checked the stalls, but they were empty. "Go home and take two aspirin," Mark said to the girl. "Drink plenty of water."

"Thank you," she said, with a small, polite voice. Mark saw then that she was hardly more than a teenager, a sheep in wolf's clothing.

In the men's room, Mark had the impression that he had stepped into an El Greco painting. The bathroom was lit by a single red bulb, and by the wrinkled red wires of space heaters. The room was stifling. Mark saw the shadowed figures of about a dozen men leaning against the tiled walls. Many had taken their shirts off, and tied them around their waists. Their skin was red with the lights, and the men glowed. Every tortured nook of their rib cages was sharply defined. Their breastplates and cheekbones and shoulders and fierce, knotted elbows stood out, painfully, achingly. Their heads looked too large to support, and seemed to wobble on their thin, strained necks. Mark saw that one man had a canister of oxygen on a pull cart, and plastic tubes in his nostrils. His chest was covered in sores. The man's hair was colorless, thin, standing up with static, swaying slightly, catching the red light. He stared at Mark, the spooky, grievous, incriminating stare that only the walking dead could manage. Mark had treated dozens of patients who were dying exactly these deaths. In the hospital they had seemed to belong, their illness in no way extraordinary. But now Mark was startled. He had never imagined these patients' lives, had never envisioned them as citizens of the world, had never really seen the hellish rooms they suffered in, together, during the last nights of their lives.

Farther back in the room, Mark saw that several men were dancing to the muffled beat of the club's music. They leaned against one another, barely moving. They held drinks in their hands in clear plastic cups, the liquid trembling with the pulse of the music. A row of urinals gleamed on the far wall. Even they were red. All was red in that room.

Then Mark saw from the corner of his eye a flash of blue. It was Robby, dancing with another man. Or rather, he was standing awkwardly, his hands at his sides, swaying slightly, while a dying man, shirtless, had his arms draped around Robby's neck. Robby's face with frozen with panic, and he was shaking slightly, like a caught rabbit.

"Excuse me," Mark said, walking toward them. "That's my brother." He put his arm around Robby. The man who had been dancing with Robby stepped back. Mark saw that he was not so bad off, yet. The man's hair was thin, and his face drawn, but his eyes were still normal. He hadn't yet developed the knowing stare of the dead.

"Let's go, buddy," Mark said, and led Robby out of the room. Robby was terrified. He stood with his hands in his pockets, shuffling his feet, fighting tears. "I want Ellie," he said, and looked at Mark pleadingly. It was the first time that Robby and Mark had been alone together, without her.

"Me, too," Mark said. He took Robby by the hand and lead him down the hall. "Let's find Ellie," Mark said. "Let's go home."

They circled the club again and again. Robby seemed to think it was a game. He called out for Ellie, mischievously, as though she were hiding. Mark had the fleeting urge to hit him. He pulled roughly at Robby's arm, dragging him through the crowded room. "Don't you get it?" he said. "This isn't a joke." He imagined Ellie in a dark corner, injured, needing help. "I'm going crazy here," he yelled.

"Why don't you check the car," Robby said, matter-of-factly. "She's in the car. Dad said always go to the car. When we're lost. Always go to the car."

Mark was furious. He imagined Ellie leaving the club without him, walking to the car by herself to find Robby. It was absurd to think that she would have reverted to an old family rule, one that Mark wasn't even aware of. It was absurd to think that Robby— simple, hopeless Robby—would know her better.

Outside of the club, the cold air was shocking. Mark took a deep, hopeful breath, and started for the car. Robby trudged behind, making deliberate prints in the stiff snow. "Always go to the car," he kept saying, imitating Ellie. "Put your hat on." He pulled his hat on. "Always follow the rules."

The protesters swayed on the opposite sidewalk, holding their signs. They were singing, in that thin, dissonant loveliness of amateurs. It was "Silent Night," one of Mark's favorites. He was not religious, but he had always liked the calm of that song. He had often thought, when he heard it, that he wouldn't mind dying listening to that song, alone in his bed, staring out a window at a single, leafless tree.

From a block away, Mark saw that the car was alone in the lot, a snow-covered mound underneath the slanting pink glow of a streetlight. The snow was falling furiously. The cuffs of Mark's pants were crusted with ice. He remembered that it had snowed like this when he and Ellie had visited her father. They had made the trip only once, to announce their marriage, six months after the ceremony. Ellie had wanted to see her brother, to tell him in person that she was married and about to have a baby. They were only supposed to stay for dinner, but they had been trapped overnight by a storm. Eight inches had fallen in the course of the afternoon, and Ellie felt divinely doomed.

Her family lived in Maine, in a small house that was heated only by fireplaces and a wood burning stove. The house was lined with books. Ellie's father had installed built-in bookshelves along every wall of the house, even in the kitchen, and the house was entirely insulated with paperbacks. Mr. Franklin had greeted Mark warmly, shaking his hand and smiling. He didn't seem concerned that his daughter had married a virtual stranger. He was a quiet man who spent his life in his den, reading, and making sketches of cathedrals in his notebook. He collected clocks, and sat all day among a comforting symphony of ticks and chimes. In every room, pendulums swung and dials turned and cuckoos burst forth from tiny doors.

The entire visit, Mark had only one extended conversation with Mr. Franklin, discussing his favorite books. He was a great lover of classics, like *War and Peace* and *A Tale of Two Cities* and *Crime and Punishment*. When he spoke of these books, Ellie's father stroked his beard fondly and made precise adjustments to the position of his eyeglasses. He recited several plotlines, sitting at the edge of his seat, gesturing with his hands. But Mr. Franklin was phlegmatic on nearly every other subject. When Mark spoke of his residency, and the trauma he saw each day as an ER doctor, Mr. Franklin stared absently out the window. He didn't listen to a word Mark said.

Neither had Robby. When Ellie had explained she was married, Robby clung to her. He sobbed, his head on her chest, and begged for Ellie to marry him, too. Robby glared at Mark. Ellie held her brother, stroked his hair, his back, his hands. She held up his palms and traced her finger across them. Robby's palms, instead of being marked with slanting lines, had a solitary horizontal crease running across them. It was one of the classic signatures of Down's. Mark had only seen it before in textbooks.

Mark sensed that they were a family that lived by strict rules, never straying from routine. They had settled comfortably into their respective roles. Ellie did the work of her dead mother, cooking and washing and keeping up the house. Her father worked as a mail carrier, and returned home in the evenings to settle down with his books. Robby needed constant care. He had doctor's appointments and part-time jobs and special classes to be driven to. He wanted Ellie to be with him at every moment, watching television, sleeping, eating, even bathing. His functioning was limited. He had to operate within a strict system of rules, rising at the same time every day and doing the same things. Frustrated, Ellie had run off to college without even telling Robby that she was leaving. College had been strange for her. She had hated the freedom, the uncertainty. She had longed for order, for structure, and had found it, Mark supposed, in marriage.

Later that night, when Mr. Franklin and Robby were asleep, Mark pressed Ellie for details about her former life with her family. She shrugged, wandered away. But there were so many things Mark wanted to know. He asked about the elaborate locks on the doors. On the front and back doors there were five deadbolts, each controlled by a different key. "What's all this about?" Mark had asked, flicking the locks open and closed. "Is this some kind of dangerous town?"

"It's Robby," Ellie explained. "He's a sleepwalker." For years he had made a habit of wandering out of the house at night while Ellie and her father were asleep. Several times the police had called, saying they found Robby walking along Route 1, a shoulderless road famous for car accidents. Ellie confessed that even in her college dorm room, two hundred miles away, she had woken some nights in terror, afraid she had left the doors unlocked.

"Always lock the doors," Robby said now. "Always wear your seatbelt. Always look before crossing the street."

As they crossed the street, Mark wasn't sure what he would find. He thought that perhaps Ellie had run away, as suddenly as she had appeared. Perhaps she had left Mark alone to care for Robby. This was, after all, a world where people abandoned each other, where loved ones were always finding new and strange ways to hurt one another. Then again, Mark thought, maybe his job was getting to him. Outside of the ER, maybe things weren't so bad. Perhaps his wife was simply waiting for him in the car, wanting nothing more than to return home and fall asleep together, in their bed, where they could be alone, and sheltered. It was possible.

The night was dark, but Mark saw the impression of a single set of footprints crossing the street. They seemed to him small and dainty as a doe's. He tracked them to the car, and stood for a moment, smiling, before he brushed a thin layer of snow from the passenger window. He saw, in the pink light that beamed down from the street lamp, that Ellie was asleep in the car, her head resting against the window, her mouth parted slightly. He saw her short curls—her awful, darling curls—pressed against the window. She glowed in that pink light, a light that wrapped around her like a warm coat, a light that gave her life.

II

Sir Karl LaFong or Current Resident

He is a heartbreak of a brother, a lusty sleeper, a yawner, an eye-rubber, a stretcher, a sniffler—a person who sleeps in his clothes and goes to work unchanged. He is skinny and slouchy in ill-fitting corduroys and stained T-shirts, in droopy socks and thin-soled shoes. He is the over-aged captain of a remote-control racecar, a sidewalk juggler, and the lonely champion-score-holder of all local pinball machines. He is the adopted black child of white, former-leftists who have raised him, as a kind of social protest, in a conservative white town. He is the child of parents who have changed over the years, parents who switched from civil liberty to corporate law and took up with Volvos, who began to investigate tax shelters and retirement plans—parents who joined the city council and the PTA and eventually the Republican party, without for an instant acknowledging the slightest mutation. More than any of these things, my brother is the Junk Mail General of the United States, having filled out, with fictional names, hundreds of postage-paid magazine inserts and consumer warranty questionnaires, and having dialed the toll-free numbers on television advertisements, requesting complimentary brochures on Mormonism, stainless steel knife sets,

ice-cream makers, wrinkle-free slacks, low-interest loans, miniature deep fryers, and run-free panty hose. We receive mail for a
thousand different people, each more outrageously named than
the last, each the invention of my brother. My parents named him
Ephram, the first of their mistakes.

I am the child my parents thought they could never have. A
biological quirk, the sullen young daughter of gray-haired near-
retirees. I am the sole heir of a priggish and Puritan family name:
Agnes Mildred. We are a family of practical jokes and suffered
consequences.

The summer I am seventeen, and Ephram twenty-one, is the
summer we lose him. Ephram has lived contentedly in his bedroom
for his entire life, in the coldest corner of my parents' house, his
walls postered with a dozen black-and-white likenesses of his closest and favorite friend—W. C. Fields, dressed as the juggling
tramp. Ephram's books, thousands of them, are piled in the closet,
in the drawers of his dresser, under his bed, and on the thin lip of his
windowsill. He has lived this way, and seems destined to live this
way, always—alone and reading, surrounded by a bounty of famous
sneers. He stomps through the house at seven each morning, returning from his dark, neon-bordered, Plexiglas-shielded shift at
our town's all-night gas station. He trails boot prints of oil across the
kitchen floor. He leaves cellophane and aluminum candy wrappers
on the table as he empties his pockets, counting and straightening
the fistful of small bills he has collected from weary drivers who
prefer to have their gas pumped by a hunched and Afroed attendant. He places half of his nightly earnings on the table—a form
of rent—and leaves the kitchen, finally, with only a short greeting
to my parents. "Sam, Betty," he says, nodding to each, though these
are not my parents' names. He leaves us to our hot, balanced break-
fasts, our tart mouthfuls of grapefruit juice, our silence and averted
glances. He leaves us to envy his modest pocketful of independence.
He leaves us to breathe in his flammable smell.

My father clears his throat and continues with the newspaper, the blinding columns and abbreviations of the financials, lined across the page like work ants. My mother slices her circle of sausage, pierces a piece with her fork. She is embarrassed in her apron and pink plastic hair-rollers. Impossibly, she is surprised each morning to find the crescents of oil left on the kitchen floor, as if they are the first-discovered tracks of a mysterious, long-extinct animal. She wipes the floor with a tissue that she keeps balled in the sleeve of her nightgown, a lingering habit of hers, though Ephram and I are long past the age of needing our noses wiped.

Odd mornings, very rarely, Ephram will stand behind my chair, tuck my hair behind my ears, and lean down, his face right in mine, upside down, and he will kiss me on the mouth, so quick and chapped that it seems we never touched. "Agnes," he'll say, smiling, speaking my actual name. These are the only times that Ephram returns my gaze. His eyes are a marvel, and he tends to keep them downcast. They are slightly different colors. One is grayish brown, and the other is brighter, resinous, the color of tree sap.

My parents—guilty and flustered, having adopted a child under one set of ideologies, and then having *changed* so (having raised Ephram to watch Dan Rather at the dinner table and even, eventually, to be a baptized member of the Catholic church)—my parents allow Ephram his freedoms. They have allowed him to shrug off the requirements of college, and its aftermath of responsible life.

And so Ephram works at the gas station, returns home each morning and sets an alarm and sleeps for eight hours, wakes in the afternoon and slips out of the house, stopping only to accuse me of picking the lock to his room and rifling through his secret files. "I have ways of telling, you little shit," he says, grabbing me from behind in a chokehold, whispering fiercely in my ear, his breath hot and smoky. "You little fucker." I do not know the contents of Ephram's files, except that they are an intricate system of catalogs and travel-sized samples, sent by mail to hundreds of his aliases. Ephram has invented a community of consumers of different ages and races, male and female, and by tracking the companies that buy mailing lists from other companies, he hopes to decipher the racist and sexist and ageist policies of major corporations. Eventually he plans to write a book—something sociological, anthropological—immaterial to me. My interest is Ephram.

When he leaves the house I follow him at a distance. I track him to his haunts. The corner hardware store, the local pizza place, and, finally, the post office—the hallowed home of his newly rented personal mailbox. This is the treasured sliver of real estate owned by Ephram and his cast of invented characters; six days a week, they receive a bounty of greetings.

This is Ephram's routine, and I follow it greedily. I am hungry for sightings. I want to collect the curious data of his life—of posture and wingspan and language, the eccentric habits of mating and preening and sleeping, of diet and self-defense that are particular to this rare species.

Ephram at fifteen: He asks, for his birthday, to be taken to Harvard Square and left alone on the sidewalk, by the newspaper stand. He loads a guitar case with bowling pins. It is April and Ephram is dressed insufficiently for the cold. There is still snow on the ground in patches. The grass, snow-sopped for months, is limp and detached at its roots, like a bad toupee. It is Ephram and my father and me, loaded in the car. We park and walk him to the corner. There is an awkward minute or two where Ephram examines every magazine at the vendor's stand, an impossible variety. We all shuffle our feet, our eyes looking between magazine covers and passersby. Students stroll past in home-knit caps, their knapsacks slung casually and wearily over their shoulders. Their faces are young and white. They are pink in the cheek. They puff glamorously on clove cigarettes and leave us in an exotic, fragrant cloud. The streets are busy with traffic. Every third car or so is a brightly colored Volkswagen, sputtering past, trailing a dark swirl of exhaust.

A tweed-jacketed, spectacle-wearing professor walks up to the newsstand, gives his name, and says, "I have some *German period-*

icals reserved," wiggling his eyebrows and speaking in an accent I have since come to recognize as the tone and meter of academic self-satisfaction. The vendor rings up the magazines and the professor flips through them. On the covers there are pictures of spread-legged naked women who are sticking sausage links in their vaginas and eyeing the cameraman lustily. "DIOS MIO!" reads one tabloid headline. There is a grainy photograph of Princess Diana in a bikini, thigh high in tropical surf.

"Welp," says Ephram. "See you in two hours."

"Okay, sport," says our father, and punches Ephram in the shoulder. He has taken to punching Ephram half-heartedly ever since Ephram bought a thrift-store Army jacket. The private's name, Gentry, is still stitched over the jacket's left pocket. "Oh, look," our father said, when he first saw it. "Conclusive evidence that gentry *did* fight in Vietnam." My father was one of many graduate students who had eluded the draft. Now he pulls the hood of my coat over my head and ties it. He is fond of tending to me unnecessarily during awkward moments in conversation.

"Back in two hours."

My father and I walk off, disappearing around the corner. Of course we return moments later, and position ourselves in the window seat of a diner. We watch Ephram standing there, on the corner, bewildered by traffic. He looks around in all directions. He wipes his palms on the back of his legs, every so often, and stares at his guitar case. Finally he opens the case, and we see its brilliant red lining stretched open on the sidewalk like a scar. Ephram crouches over his bowling pins. He stands, looks around, and begins juggling. He keeps the pins close to him, as though embarrassed to take up space. He starts breathing through his mouth, and his breath fogs. At first there are three pins, and they whirl neatly through the air in a nice, easy cross pattern. Then, using his foot, Ephram kicks a fourth pin into flight. It springs up, revolving toward him, and he catches it. For a second he is triumphant, a broad smile breaking across his face. But something in his balance is off. He had leaned back too far in his kick and he can't recover. His arms are over-stretched and a pin gets away from him. It rolls off the sidewalk and onto the street, into traffic. A Volkswagen runs over the pin and, it seems, almost overturns. The pin scatters away, across the street, and settles over the grate of a rain gutter. By then the rest of the pins have dropped, and Ephram panics after them. He gathers them to his chest, and stands, huddled. He is shivering in rust-colored corduroys and an unlined Army jacket. The pins stand out against his clothes. They are bright and polished, and they seem somehow amused by their momentary escape. Ephram settles the pins in his guitar case and walks off, across the street, to rescue the fourth. We see him bend for it, and then stand up again, empty-handed. He touches the pin with his foot, lightly, then walks away, down the street, his back turned. The pin remains on the street, looking like the last glass-bottled quart of milk on the face of the earth.

Ephram looks smaller, now. Not nearly so big, so brazen. He is thin and long-limbed and frail. He looks in need of shelter.

I stand up and gather my coat.

"Let him be," says my father, who is reading the *Globe*. "We said two hours."

Inside the diner, behind the counter, two black men are arguing jovially. They wear blue pants and white T-shirts, and white paper hats in the shape of ocean liners. One man is scraping the grill with a spatula, and the other is hunched over a meat slicer, one palm resting on a block of ham, guiding it back and forth.

"Kick my ass," says the man with the spatula. "Go ahead, kick it. I dare you."

"I been known," says the other man.

They laugh, and the man at the grill cracks open an egg. It hisses. He splits the yolk, then flips the egg. When he lifts the egg off the grill, the yolk is still dripping raw. The cook eases the egg on top of a cheeseburger. This is the house specialty.

"I lost part of my finger slicing meat," says my father. He tilts his head fancifully, and light fills the circular lenses of his eyeglasses.

"When I was their age. Look." He holds out his right index finger. There is a perfectly circular scar at the tip. "This whole piece right here, I cut it off and it fell on the floor. I just picked it up, put it back, and pressed on it very hard. Then I thought enough to adjust it so it would heal right." I look closer. He had done a nice job aligning the swirls of his fingerprint. He has always been a sensible man. "It closed right up. We couldn't afford a doctor, anyway," he says, and sighs. I tend to forget that my father had grown up horribly poor. Rats used to scurry under his bed. It was because of this, my father reasoned, that he turned out conscionable. Also for that reason, Ephram and I receive no allowance.

Here is Ephram the summer that he leaves, going about his routine for the last time. On his days off he lounges by the pool in the backyard, with his girlfriend, Gretchen, a girl from my high school who wears our long, pleated, Catholic skirts and white knee-socks with a bold flair all her own. She wears our oxford shirt tight and braless, her small breasts plainly visible to our red-faced, tactful instructors. She wears, perpetually, a smear of red lipstick, and two upturned slashes of black eyeliner. She carries a small bottle of cornstarch in her backpack and rubs it hourly over her face, tending to a shocking and cherished paleness. Ephram is part of a defiant streak of Gretchen's that has lately been the talk of the school. Gretchen and I are related by gossip. We are respectively the exceptionally wild and the exceptionally studious members of our junior class, linked by a sullen gas-station attendant. We have never actually spoken. I know Gretchen mostly by rumor. The previous fall, during the SAT tests, she had reportedly sat dramatically slumped over in a nap, cat yawning every few minutes, stretching her arms over her head, eventually making a paper airplane out of the test sheet and openly and unbelievingly launching her future in a low-flying, doomed trajectory.

Ephram first saw Gretchen's picture in the newspaper, after she was named homecoming queen. Gretchen was so beautiful that she was friendless, and I was surprised that she had won a popular vote. But her beauty was such that no one could bring himself to lie on a ballot. Ephram had clipped Gretchen's picture from the paper and carried it in his wallet. He was determined to know her.

Because Gretchen is my age there is something awkward about the whole arrangement. I try speaking their names, Gretchen and Ephram, as if they belonged together. It doesn't sound right. Never has anyone in the history of the world said "Gretchen and Ephram" without sounding like a speech therapist. But Gretchen has covered her notebook with her name, and Ephram's name, enclosed in hearts, as though they were manifest. On the last day of school, I overheard Gretchen in the lunch line, talking about her plans for the next summer, after she graduates: She and Ephram will run away to Vegas.

Weekdays, Ephram and Gretchen tread water in the deep end of my parents' pool, holding each other for the briefest intervals, before they have to break apart and move to keep afloat. They are beautiful, dark-haired creatures. They think themselves unseen.

I teach piano that summer, and read. I am a tragic moper, a snoop.

"Aggie," Ephram says, coming into the kitchen one of those afternoons, Gretchen trailing behind in nothing but her bright orange bikini. Ephram is shirtless and horribly thin. It seems the only thing holding up his shorts is the water that clings the fabric to his legs. He tracks water onto the floor, my mother's perfect floor. He grabs an apple from the refrigerator, eats it in five casual bites. "What's happening?"

"Nothing," I say, flipping through a magazine, noting the advice of beauty experts: to wet and condition one's hair before going out in the sun, to make liberal use of sunscreen, to employ a straw hat and protective lip balm. "Bored."

"Too bad," he says, heading toward his room.

"Hello, Agnes," says Gretchen, and places her hand on the top of my head. "Aggie, Aggie."

"What are you guys doing?" I say. My voice cracks and Ephram laughs.

"Hanging out. Upstairs."

"I want to see your room," I say. "Please? Please, please, please, please?" It has been years. Despite Ephram's suspicions, I have never broken his lock. I have not seen the inside of Ephram's room since it was sealed off on the eve of his high school graduation, the day he started paying rent. There could be anything in there. There could be a planetarium.

"Come on, E," says Gretchen. She walks over to him and plays with the waistband of his shorts. "Big deal."

"Please?" I say, standing up.

With Gretchen around, Ephram is in a mood. He says yes.

Perhaps I should have seen it coming. I might have known, then, by this gesture alone, that things were changing for Ephram. I had asked to see his room hundreds of times, and he had always laughed and run up the stairs, two at a time. There have been moments in my life that I've sometimes sensed that I'll never see someone again, perhaps as he's putting on his jacket or waving good-bye, jovially, with all the good faith in the world, and in a flash I can see his car stalled on train tracks, or the swerving brazenness of a drunk driver. I should have had that feeling, looking back.

But I'm not thinking of that. For now, Ephram is simply in a mood.

There are three deadbolts on Ephram's bedroom door, which he had installed immediately after his graduation ceremony. He opens the door, ushers Gretchen and me inside, and locks the door again. He is still taken with the locks. It is clear that he enjoys their snapping.

Gretchen strolls across the room and lies on the bed, sprawled dramatically. She runs her finger across her stomach and stares dreamily at the ceiling. I am in the room, interrupting something. In this room I am somehow grotesque, like an extra finger, but I can't bring myself to leave.

I want to take in all the details of Ephram's life, and I just stand there, staring. Ephram has covered over the windows with black trash bags and even at the height of summer it is dark and cool in his room. Gone is Ephram's old high school room with its musty smell, his clothes, his underwear strewn on the floor, glasses of soda—half-filled and full of dust—perched on various stacks of books. There is no trace of his formerly beloved television, left running but muted at all times, tuned to the black-and-white classic movie channel. Of the former posters on his wall, only one remains, of a young and skinny W. C. Fields, presneer, pregrog-blossom. Fields's hair is thick and wild, like Einstein's. He is dressed in tuxedo pants and a white shirt. His face is painted white, with a clownish red smear around the lips. Three crayoned stripes angle from the outer corners of each eye, toward the temple, like whiskers. Fields is juggling very neatly, precisely, the balls held close to his body, thrown in a pattern no wider than his hips. He is frowning dramatically. It is a picture of restraint, the agonizing repetition of small circles.

The walls of Ephram's room are otherwise white. Five black, three-drawer filing cabinets are lined along one wall. Ephram has constructed built-in bookshelves along the other walls, and his books are meticulously ordered, separated into paperback and hard-backs, arranged by height. His twin bed is gone, replaced with a full-sized mattress, kept on the floor, neatly covered with a white comforter. There is a padlock on the closet door. The overhead chandelier—a feature in every room of my parents' house—has been disassembled, no teary bits of crystal, no brass piping, just the plain bulb, like a podless pea, like an only child.

On the nightstand there is a clock and a phone, and a cluster of orange prescription bottles.

There is a long silence. "E," Gretchen says after a while. "Honey." And then she is taking off the top of her swimsuit. She stands up, stretches. "I need to use the bathroom." She pads topless down the hall. She leaves us alone.

"Okay?" Ephram says. "Seen enough?" I'm still just inside the doorway, still taking it all in. He's pushing me out.

"Wait," I say. We haven't really spoken in years. Not since Ephram took his night job.

Ephram has me pinned against the door, leaning against me, his hands on my shoulders. It is the same posture I have seen him take with a tricky pinball machine, pressing all his weight on its corners. The look he gives me is one I haven't seen before. There's something wrong with his eyes. One is steady and focused, and the other seems slightly unhinged, slightly drifting. It causes me to place my hand on the back of his neck, to leave it there, and we are standing like that for a long time, breathing each other's warm breath.

We are confused. Gretchen has been walking around topless, and it has confused us. The air is sensual and we seem touched on all sides, especially standing so close, there are things we want from each other: to talk, to roam in each other's heads for a little. We want to be loved.

I was betrothed at an early age to Freddie Fontana. Freddie and I were the promising children of an elite, exclusive tribe of suburban doctors and lawyers. Our parents worked out the terms of our eventual marriage over dinner parties and business lunches. Sometimes I imagined that there was a signed contract; my father was Freddie's father's lawyer. But likely the arrangement was significantly more subtle, more sly. It was understood that the Fontanas would sponsor me, at the age of six, in my school's read-a-thon; my father would in turn clip out newspaper articles about Freddie's phenomenal little-league pitching skill and tape them to the refrigerator; when my mother was working late, Mrs. Fontana would watch me and Ephram, saying all the while how she always wanted a girl.

Freddie was two years older than me. Growing up, he was Ephram's best friend, although they grew apart in high school. Freddie had a broad, oily face, a freckled nose, and thick sandy hair cut straight across his forehead. His eyes were coolly blue. He wore tube socks and sneakers with his dressy school uniform. He had trouble keeping his shirt tucked in and his tie was always pulled loose. What saved Freddie for respectability was that his father was a prominent surgeon at Boston General, and his mother was the daughter of a Congressman. Therefore, Freddie knew things that other boys his age didn't: the names of the best resorts in Vail, the best hotels in Tuscany, and the worst nightclubs in New York City. He knew the phone numbers at the Kennedy compound. He knew the fair asking price of a slightly used Jaguar, his sixteenth birthday present. He was vaguely interested in science and baseball and poetry and film, like any prep student. He was unexceptional in every way, except for his guaranteed future.

As teenagers, Freddie and I were encouraged to accompany each other to dances. Our parents imagined our bodies touching only through the flimsy connection of a shared plastic straw, speared in a scoop of ice cream in a drugstore float.

In fact I had lost my virginity to Freddie the previous winter, after a Catholic school dance, in his bedroom while his parents were watching television in the next room. During sex, our first sex, we heard the *Tonight Show*'s theme music starting up after each set of commercials, the applause of the crowd. That night there was an audience member whose laughter stood out above all the rest, louder and longer and stranger, like the laugh of an asthmatic donkey. It was the laugh of a middle-aged accountant, an overweight and buck-toothed dentist, a glasses-wearing music teacher with a misbuttoned shirt. The laugh of a man who still lived in the bedroom of his parents' house, a man whose underwear was hung weekly on the backyard clothesline for all the world to see. A man in town for a conference, a man who had never before been out late and never would again. He laughed and laughed. Everything was funny to him. Even the torturous movements of teenage sex. I thought so much about this man, imagining the bogginess of his lonely life, that Freddie's clumsiness seemed immaterial, like the irritating flutter of an insect, like the pointless elbowing of siblings in the backseat of the family car.

Afterward, Freddie was overcome with emotion. He confided to me his fears about not getting into Harvard, and the connections his father might have to employ if he were turned down, the excellent quality of his grades weighed against his mediocre performance on the SATs, and didn't Ephram get a perfect score, and didn't he get into Harvard, and what had happened to him, why had he changed so much, and why was he working in a gas station, and didn't my parents want to kill him. I could tell that the distance that had grown between Ephram and Freddie over the past few years really bothered him. "Not perfect," I said. "Near perfect. He missed one vocabulary question." This seemed to make Freddie feel better. I was, I realized then, a person in the business of pleasing others.

Ephram first started to collect junk mail when he was in high school. When I returned home from grade school, he would already be sitting on the living room floor with a stack of brochures, scribbling on a legal pad. He was secretive about his work, but occasionally showed me some of his favorites. "Look," he'd say, holding a tiny bottle of hair spray. "They actually sent this to a fake person I made up. *Miss Claire Marie Cantelope.*" He'd smile at the address label, showing his two giant front teeth. "I'm going to have Clair Cantelope write them a thank-you." And he would, thrilled at the prospect of inventing her signature, her loopy handwriting and over-polite phrasing. He invented her whole life, her age, her bitter divorce, her recent experience with a bad perm, her dislike of Dan Rather.

I, too, have the impulse to invent and to keep records. There are a number of things that are stuck in my head, at sixteen, that won't be rid of, images of people I know or don't know, regardless, who I have caught sight of perhaps on the subway or sidewalk, people who are intent on something and don't think themselves observed: a fat elderly woman in a raincoat adjusting the green sweater of her

Scottish terrier, one triangular flap of her umbrella loose and flapping in the wind; a man sitting at a picnic bench in the park, toothless, his mouth curled in like an apple without a stem, slowly and
confusedly punching the buttons of a handheld children's video
game; a child standing apart from other children at a Saturday session of free community tennis lessons, wearing in the dead of summer a white turtleneck and blue corduroys, an overly large straw
hat, and black-framed glasses, swinging his wooden racket faintly
and sadly and out of rhythm; my parents, many years ago, in the
middle of a party they held at the house, my father adjusting the
wayward strap of my mother's bra, their open and smiling mouths,
their white teeth glistening, wet with scotch; and Ephram, bent
over a book, framed in the yellow light of the plastic booth at the gas
station, a booth built for one, a small, bright island in the center of
the rows of gas pumps—I have seen Ephram at work, as I'm driven
home from a night of baby-sitting, his head down, his face hidden
and only his hair visible, his giant halo of hair, like a turtle's shell,
and he looks curled into himself, hopelessly coiled inward, cold in
his thin blue jacket and alone, alone. Worse than the fate of living
with these pictures, these people, is the possibility of forgetting
them, these brief slivers of time you've seized and copied so precisely. I see what Ephram wants.

My entire life I have been a meticulous and patient planner. A
model of self-control. I have kept up with schoolwork, a quiet, mus-
ing student, never raising my hand in class, feigning shyness, but
allowing myself to be called on, smiling faintly and knowingly at
my teachers, wearing my skirt long, as it is meant to be worn, instead of rolled at the waist, keeping my wildly curly hair pulled
back out of my face, leaving my lips neglected and chapped, bowing
my head dutifully at morning prayer, acting as class president and
tennis captain, teaching Sunday school to five year olds, helping at
the church's Oktoberfests and spring bazaars, contentedly sweeping
a paper cone around the cotton candy machine, or standing over a

charcoal flame grilling a hundred links of sausage, I have done all of this patiently, peacefully, planning all the while to be accepted to a prestigious college, preferably Harvard, an indulgent place in which to go wild and drunken. All of this is a year within my reach. I try to contain myself. I spend my weekends with other of St. Mary's reputable girls, renting movies and eating popcorn, consulting astrological charts for romantic advice, giggling at mildly suggestive jokes, wondering aloud if any of our teachers has ever had sex, and with whom. I swear with the rest of them to be friends forever, knowing full well I'll leave in a year, leave letters unanswered, and never return. I have it figured.

I had assumed that Freddie would do the same when he left for Harvard. Instead there was his first triumphant trip home, at Thanksgiving, and then Christmas. He returned home again for spring break, sick with the flu. I saw him on each of these occasions. We had conversations about the various clubs that Freddie had enrolled in, and the number of Harvard Square restaurants and bars that were open late, and how in each of these places one could purchase beer without an ID and listen to ten different languages being spoken at surrounding tables, as though one were in Babylon.

When Freddie returns home after his freshman year, we go into the city on Saturday nights. Each week we tour a different section. We tour the historic churches and state buildings, the jazz clubs, the museums, the drag shows, the blue-collar bars. Freddie has friends everywhere. They wave exuberantly to each other across crowded rooms, a recognition between tanned faces and white teeth and calfskin loafers and diamond-studded money clips. We are often lost in the city, though Freddie darts in and out of traffic with a riled smugness that always puts us back on track.

The week before schools starts up, Freddie and I are walking in Boston's North End—a tangled neighborhood of narrow streets lined with Italian bakeries and restaurants and double-parked Chevy Monte Carlos. All along the sidewalks are small, round tables that have spilled out from the cafés and ice-cream parlors, and people are sitting outside, smoking, sipping three-layered drinks, and laughing uproariously. It is the effect that most television advertisers go for but never quite achieve. The wealthy sailor in his white pants and blue blazer, his sockless feet in loafers, surrounded by admiring women. It is all here. It is still light enough to see, the sky sort or colorless, streaked with pink clouds. The street lamps have blinked on, and it will be dark in a matter of minutes. Freddie has bought, rather brutishly, a rose from a sidewalk vendor. "Keep the change," Freddie had said, thrusting a five into the man's hand and snatching the flower out of its plastic bucket, not wanting to finish the trade. The stem of the rose is dripping wet. Its thorns are green, its head small and tightly closed, barely fragrant. We walk. Freddie is scanning the streets nervously, hunting for a restaurant he frequented last year in college. "Wait'll you meet Bruno," he says, searching for a casual tone. "The owner. He's great." My fear is that we will meet Bruno, and that Freddie will embarrass himself with false camaraderie.

"Oh, look," a woman is suddenly saying, pointing at us. "Look at the beautiful couple." She is old, her hair in curlers, and she is wearing a short, flowered, snap-front apron as a dress. Her feet are in rose-colored slippers. She is sitting on the front steps of her apartment building, surveying passersby. "You two win the prize for the evening," she calls to us. I notice she is toothless. "You two are truly in love." We smile, wave, walk past. "I have a gift for these things," she yells. And I know instantly she has entered my file of remembered people, of those so confused they are hopeless. *"Strangers in the night, exchanging glances,"* the woman is singing now, her voice cracking and growing distant. *"Doobie doobie doo."*

This woman reminds me of my grandmother, my father's mother, who lived alone in the city for years, in a tiny, third-floor apartment that I only saw a handful of times. My father brought her to our house for holidays, and dropped her off afterward. Her apartment was, our father reported, so cluttered with cats and junk mail that it was impossible for more than two people to navigate.

The light is changing quickly now, and people look unlike themselves, softened, gentled, slow-moving. It is as though everyone is drunk from the same cup of bluish liquor, and they are calmed. The people sitting at the sidewalk tables are leaning back luxuriously in their chairs, swirling their spaghetti lovingly around the tines of their forks. There are clusters of collared priests, of teenagers, of businessmen and of housewives in pleated tennis skirts. There are most especially businessmen, most particularly a group of five huddled around a small table. One of whom is the spit and image of Ephram, if Ephram were to wear a suit and tie. It is a gray suit with a nice sheen. The shirt is pressed and white, the tie a bold, brilliant yellow flecked with blue. This man is breathing snobbishly through his long nose, swirling a snifter. His legs are crossed, his shoes long and black and polished, like gondolas. One leg is extending so far out onto the sidewalk that it almost trips me.

"Hey," says Freddie, when he sees I have stopped. "Hey, it's your brother." He gives my arm a backhanded slap. The man regards us casually, with a raised eyebrow. He looks at Freddie, his former best friend, and then at me. He gives us a tart smile, devoid of recognition. I raise my hand halfway into a wave, then stop, my mouth open, the first syllable of greeting stuck in my throat.

I see, at that moment, that I am interrupting one of Ephram's personalities. That his personalities have moved from their cozy post office box out into the world.

Now Freddie is looking at me. I start walking, my head down, swatting away Freddie's questions.

"I hardly understand," I hear a voice say, Ephram's voice, "how I could be mistaken for that girl's brother." Then there is the laughter of men who seem to know each other.

Ephram has packaged himself as God knows what—a young entrepreneur, an inventor, a professor of mathematics at MIT, a traveling dignitary, the son of an ambassador. Perhaps in another part of town he has told a different story to dozens of women who leaned across tables and gazed at him unblinkingly with sad smiles, listening to the sorrowful history of his life as a foster child, a wrongly imprisoned former inmate, a back-alley punk-beaten victim of racial hatred in this rich, white, New England corner of our planet. All of this for the purpose of sociological research, for his treasured book.

W. C. Fields was fond of whimsical aliases. Many of his films credit such men as Charles Snavely and Mahatma Kane Jeeves as screenwriters. Fields delighted in naming the characters he invented. There was Larson E. Whipsnade, the rogue, and Og Oggleby, suitor to Field's daughter. There were Mr. and Mrs. Bissonet. There was A. Pismo Clam.

Fields was rumored to keep bank accounts under different names, in different cities. He was stingy with money, having grown up the poor son of a drunk. Fields's wife and son, left behind in Philadelphia, received little of his earnings.

Other trivia: Once, when asking to open a bank account at a small, country branch, Fields was referred to an account manager named Miss Clapsaddle. "Miss Clapsaddle," muttered Fields. "Indeed." Thereafter, whenever Fields entered the bank, he called out for Miss Clapsaddle with utmost glee.

During the war, Fields once told a friend that he kept fifty thousand dollars in a bank in Berlin, "in case that little bastard wins."

My mother has adopted seventeen children in Micronesia. It is a habit that escalates in the weeks before Ephram leaves. She sends money to various foundations, in return for which she receives pictures of her sponsored children. Nearly all of the children pose for their pictures in the same posture. They stand with their arms locked behind their backs, smiling at their toes, their stomachs thrust out. It is the posture of shyness, of confusion, and my mother adores it. "Look at these sweet innocent babies," she says. Many of them wear eyeglasses in oversized frames that have to be secured to their heads with string. Now and then, when I return home from piano lessons, my mother will ask me into the kitchen to show me a picture of my latest brother, taped to the refrigerator. "Meet Joseph," she says. "He's five and he's color-blind."

My mother is anguished. She lives entirely outside of herself, absorbed in the trials of others. She pays no attention to her own health or appearance. She has cut her hair short, and she curls it tight to her head. She has sworn off makeup. Each night she returns home from the office, where she has sued and settled and counter-sued all day, and she changes immediately into her bathrobe, pours a twenty-ounce gin and tonic, and settles in front of the television. She watches dramas. She loves to mire herself in fabricated despair.

My mother hasn't cooked dinner in over five years. In the mornings, sober and restored, she cooks a hot breakfast.

I had heard my parents arguing that summer about my mother's new children. "They're *our* children," she shouted once, at which my father laughed. Amidst all of this, my parents only had one fight about Ephram. I was in the living room, playing the "Pathetique" sonata, when my father started yelling. "Jesus Christ!" he said, and banged his fist on something. "Jesus *Fucking* Christ, Muriel. Grow the *fuck* up." His voice was fully, entirely engaged. I had never heard anything like it. Then his footsteps were coming closer. When he walked past the living room, on his way out, I sat frozen at the piano, rigid, my fingers still poised over the keys.

My mother came into the living room, sobbing. She blew her nose on the hem of her sweatshirt. "My poor little baby," she said, and slumped on the couch. "You know," she said, "it's just because he loves him. He can't stand him working at that horrible gas station. With people driving by, people we know, you know? It's humiliating." She didn't seem to notice me. She seemed to be talking to herself.

Once, in the waiting room of a doctor's office, I read in a women's magazine that children with unusual names were prone to success-ful adulthoods. Oddly named children grew up to be chemists, astronauts, inventors, and architects. These were solitary professions, thought to be entered as refuges for withdrawn outcasts. Children made unique and outstanding by their names became studious loners. Parents should consider themselves warned or encouraged, as the case may be.

I believe Ephram to be one of those geniuses. Though he is not flourishing in a lucrative profession, he is still a creator, a collector, still an important thinker. He is gifted with something.

One afternoon Ephram emerged from his room, having just woken from a dream. He walked into the kitchen, rubbing his eyes. "Hey, Aggie," he said. "Listen to this." His dream was about a mall developer named Stan, who was installing a giant set of marble steps at a mall's entrance on its opening day, and who was also giving away a Jeep and a safari trip as part of the opening festivities. "So Stan says, in my dream, right?" Ephram is standing, his legs spread apart, his hands held out as though he were signaling to stop traffic. "Okay, Stan says to the crowd as he's about to cut the ribbon to the mall entrance with the new steps, he says, 'That's one mall step for Stan, one lion Jeep for mankind.'"

A few months later, during a Shakespeare kick, Ephram claimed to have dreamed in iambic pentameter.

After that night in Boston I am chilly to Ephram. For the first time I stop watching him and waiting for his return. Ephram and Gretchen spend an unusual amount of time at the house, sitting at the kitchen table, writing on napkins and whispering conspiratorially. I venture into the kitchen now and then, for a snack, but I don't linger like I used to. I pretend interest in the piano. I hope they hear my music, the mournful and dissonant concerto I'm composing.

When Ephram calls my name one afternoon I think it is an invitation. "Oh, Agnes," he yells, jokingly formal. "Agnes Mildred Clayson!"

I follow his voice. He is standing on the front porch, holding the front door open, leaning inside. Even though it is ninety degrees, he is wearing his blue gas-station pants and jacket and his blue knit gloves, his favorite clothes. If I get too close, I can tell, he will instantly disappear. His car is running in the drive. I see that the passenger seat is empty, that Ephram is leaving Gretchen behind, too. I see that he has no one.

"Look," he says, turning one pocket inside out, "nothing but the clothes on my back." He smiles. His teeth are brilliant, as they have always been, but they surprise me every time I see them. It is rare that I do.

"Hey," I say, and bend over slightly, reflexively, holding my stomach, as though I've been kicked. I feel short of breath. I know what's coming. I feel myself starting to cry, something I haven't done in years. My mouth is open, so wide I feel my lips crack, and I'm looking at Ephram through tears now, and for a moment I see him so clearly I call out, a sound that isn't even a word, something in a lower language.

"Take me," I manage.

"This is not for you," he says, and fixes his dark eyes on me, and turns away.

Ephram's favorite movie scene, from W. C. Fields's *It's a Gift:* Fields plays the henpecked husband. Badgered and bludgeoned into the wee hours, he sneaks out onto the second-floor back porch, in his pajamas, in an effort to sleep. Everything goes wrong. The porch swing breaks. The neighbors make a racket. Finally, just as Fields is dozing off, a door-to-door insurance salesman shouts up to him. "Do you know a man by the name of Karl LaFong? Capitol L, small a, capital F, small o, small n, small g. LaFong! Karl LaFong!" The salesman is delighted. He is an early morning man. In his tidy hat and jacket, with his trim figure and bold, enunciated speech, the salesman represents the kind of person that Fields most despises: the kind of person who finds his own company enjoyable. Fields swaggers to the railing and growls: "No, I don't know Karl LaFong. Capital *L*, small *a*, capital *F*, small *o*, small *n*, small *g*. And if I did know Karl LaFong I wouldn't admit it!"

Ephram loved that scene. He played it again and again on his VCR. Sometimes when we spoke to him, he launched into an imitation. It got so familiar that eventually all he needed to say was "Capital L, small a," and we knew to leave him alone. We were solicitors, that sickening breed of unwanted callers.

Occasionally we received mail for Karl LaFong. Whenever Ephram saw a television advertisement for life insurance, he called for a brochure, and gave the LaFong name. It killed him that no one ever caught the joke. No insurance salesman in Tuscaloosa or Raleigh-Durham had ever seen himself as the beneficiary of a joke.

Our father, a Charlie Chaplin man, was a necessary enemy of Fields.

Before I was born, when Ephram was young, dressed in brightly striped cotton shirts and overalls, he played in the hall closet with two imaginary friends, Karly and Wally. He would play for hours, in complete darkness, speaking in three different voices. Every so often, as my mother tells it, she would knock on the closet door and ask if Ephram was home. "No, ma'am, Mrs. Clayson," said Ephram, in a high-pitched voice so unlike his own that my mother was often startled. "Is that you, Karly?" my mother would say. "Would Karly like some milk?"

"Yes, please, Mrs. Clayson, ma'am," said Ephram. "Just leave it on the floor, please. I'll come get it."

My mother never knew how Ephram came to use the word "ma'am." She was, at the time, a staunch feminist who did not allow such words in her house.

Later, my father would claim that Karly and Wally were the first signs of my brother's illness. My father spoke so assuredly of Ephram's "disease," while it was never certain to me that Ephram was ill in any way, but something much simpler. He was different. He was sad.

Ephram is out there somewhere. He is sleeping open-mouthed at a subway station without a dollar in his pocket. Or he is juggling on a street corner, his hat upturned on the sidewalk, empty of change. He is keeping three pins in the air, the familiar toss-up and catch, the comfort of an old habit. He is out there somewhere.

We are all in danger of falling. Each day that we are neatly and swiftly rescued is a kind of gift.

The Great Americans

He knew in the beginning that he was moving into an apartment building with James Dean and Mark Twain, and that he was, co-incidentally, Theodore Roosevelt, but he did not know that with their run-down, one-bedroom apartments and their diets of cold cereal and canned soda, with their laundry piled on the floor, their shirtsleeves and pant legs slumped in the desperate sprawl of dying men, with their mailboxes full of catalogs flaunting the glossy lawn chairs and gas grills they would never own, and with all of their hopes for different futures locked away in dark rooms, drying up like forgotten plants—he did not know until later that they were all great Americans.

This was during a strange season, when Ted was suffering from insomnia and bouts of heightened senses, and recovering from divorce in an apartment the size of a hospital room. This was the season when he was making the best money of his life as a night janitor at the local university, and also when the campus was over-run with a circus of strange performers, evangelists and jugglers and accordion players, and, most notably, a famed shoe-snatcher who prowled for women's footwear. All of these affairs were helplessly related. They were inseparable in the way that water can't be readily extracted from an apple, or blood from flesh, inseparable by the same logic that shafted Shylock.

Theodore Roosevelt had never been a noticeable man. He had brown hair and brown eyes, a straight nose, and a square jaw. He was lean and slightly taller than average, but not in such a way that he stood out in a crowd. Ted's name was his life's curse, in that it brought his dullness to people's attention. He had none of the boisterous charm of his namesake. He was not a hunter or a horseback rider, and he did not wear white suits with a flourishing mustache. Ted's parents had done their best to take advantage of their distinguished last name. They had named their second son Franklin, hoping that their boys would become great men. Ted was, he knew, a disappointment.

Ted's greatness had taken its time, and when it came to him it was in a form that cost him his job and his wife. The greatness started with short-lived attacks of perception, during which things were more intensely themselves. It was like walking around without skin. Things started slowly. At first, while watching silent movies, Ted thought he could hear the whisk of a mime's coat sleeve, and he felt a slickness on his fingers when famous villains twisted their oily moustaches. When Ted listened to music he could hear the swiveling hips of back-up singers as they swayed back and forth, waiting for their cues. Eventually Ted thought he heard the snap of earthworms tugged from his lawn by hungry birds. Sometimes he thought he could hear loose change jingling in the trousers of old men the world over, and he sensed the collective embarrassment of all the world's misbuttoned shirts and unzipped flies. As he sat in the house each day that summer, pretending to prepare for the upcoming school year, he heard the slow, stalking approach of the ice-cream truck from a mile off, its tinkling music so faint and so maddening. That summer Ted was also sure that he detected an unfamiliar cologne on the collars of his wife's blouses. He stood in her closet each morning after she left for work, holding each blouse to his nose, breathing dutifully and sadly, like a bloodhound assigned to the tracking of a kidnapped child.

These attacks were nauseating to Ted, like the slow-motion stair climbing of horror movie actors. He never knew what would happen. In late summer, still a married professional, Ted had an attack so terrifying that he wound up crawling out of a meeting. It was the beginning of the semester, and the chancellor of Baxter Community College, where Ted taught American History, was hosting the annual orientation session. The meeting was held in a wide room with long tables arranged in rows. Ted had made the mistake of sitting in the back, far from the door, hoping to be ignored for forty minutes. But the meeting carried on for hours. Visitors kept arriving, tiptoeing quietly into the room, waiting to explain the importance of whatever collegiate program they were members of—the Language Lab, the Cultural Enrichment Office, the Johnny Carson Appreciation Society. Ted's attack started with the gleam of the chancellor's belt buckle, which flashed every so often as it caught the light. Ted realized, in the blinding glare of that belt buckle, that he was ten years out of college with nothing to his name but a Master's in American History and a modest life insurance policy and a closet full of plaid shirts and knit ties and fake leather belts creased at the slightly expanding intervals of his waistline. Ted slipped out of his chair and sat on the floor. He could see the scuff marks on the vinyl-covered briefcases of his colleagues, the thinning soles of their shoes, the threads hanging from the cuffs of their pants, the patches of fabric at the knees and elbows of their clothes that were faded and worn from years of washing. He saw the clutter in their purses, the gum wrappers and miniature bottles of knockoff perfume, the protruding tips of their cheap ballpoint pens. He could smell the petty change in their pockets. The faculty made eighteen-thousand dollars a year, if tenured, although most made only nine-thousand as part-time adjunct faculty, and they ate macaroni and cheese from a box every night, grading papers at the kitchen table with the belief that one day they would be promoted.

Above all there was the stench of desperation, and Ted felt himself choking.

Just then a group of women in saris entered the room, and it was so overcrowded that the women were forced to stand in front of the door. When Ted saw that the exit was blocked he knew he had to get out. He gathered up his handouts and pamphlets and started crawling. He was, like a dog, in a position to sniff feet that had been let out of shoes and to suffer the sight of the pale crescents of skin that had been unbuttoned from the grips of tight-fitting slacks. He kept crawling. People were leaning over and moving their bags, moving aside their chairs. Ted focused only on the women in saris. One sari had small circular mirrors sewn at the hem, and they swayed slightly, reflecting the carpet and the overhead light, and the miniature gazing faces of all the world's people, Ted thought, who might currently be examining themselves in mirrors. He thought of a dentist's mirror, and he felt plaque settling along his gum line at that very instant. When Ted reached the door, the chancellor stopped lecturing. He glared at Ted.

"Sorry," Ted said, and nodded gravely. He was on his hands and knees. A thousand years ago, he thought, floors were swept and cows milked and stones set in the crowns of kings by men like himself. He stood and opened the door and ran out, ran all the way to his car, sped home, and ate an entire bag of potato chips.

All of this took place in a southern college town, a town that revolved entirely around the state university, which was nearly two hundred years old. At the town's center stood the university's grandiose brick buildings and green lawns and expansive flowerbeds. The surrounding neighborhoods were generally reserved for students and faculty, and the town extended from there in circles of declining prosperity. At the farthest edge stood Baxter Community College, whose campus consisted of a dozen renovated trailers. Ted had lived with his wife in a small development adjacent to Baxter. It was a neighborhood of ranch homes built in the 'seventies. They were houses with small bedrooms and single baths, with wood-paneled walls and green carpeting. Each house was the same, varying only in color. And so when Ted left off teaching at Baxter and took a custodial job at the university, where he had done his graduate work, he felt that in some ways he was making a small social advancement. It turned out that university staff made twice as much as Baxter professors, plus dental.

Ted's wife was less impressed. "Did you quit or get fired?" she had asked, after his fateful attack.

"I don't know," he said.

"Then you were fired," she said. "And you're sick."

He was sick. He started keeping a file on himself, noting the dates and times and natures of each sensory episode. The file was a cross between a medical chart, a science fiction novel, and Ted's thousand-page Ph.D. dissertation on the vague topic of the history of popular culture in America, which he had abandoned after his second year of graduate school.

Mr. Roosevelt baffles science, the file began:
Not even the world's most sophisticated doctors can explain what is happening to him. It seems that Mr. Roosevelt has developed his senses to the point that he can smell fear.

Two weeks later, when Ted's wife found the file, she asked him to leave.

Now these were his mornings: Just as Ted was falling asleep, James Dean, his new neighbor, was waking. The two men shared a bedroom wall. James Dean was a simple man who liked to celebrate the arrival of each new day with loud music. He kept an LP player in his bedroom, and he played his music, Ted thought, the way other people raced cars or had sex or jumped out of airplanes. James Dean listened to the world's most desperate songs: Al Green, James Brown, Sam Cooke, and Aretha Franklin, all singing about love. James was crazy for that music. He opened his windows for all the world to hear it. It was a neighborhood quirk, like a tree growing in the middle of a road or a bright orange house. James sang along, both lead and chorus. "Try me," he sang, in a gruff imitation of James Brown. "Try me," he echoed, in the high, eager pitch of backup singers. "And your love will always be true." They were songs about making love and losing love, and other torturous habits of the human heart. James sang like he'd been there, as if he knew. Ted could hear him dancing around his room, sliding across the wood floor in his socks, occasionally slipping and falling and knocking over furniture. This was all James had ever dreamed of, his own apartment and his own music, and no one to complain.

Some days Ted couldn't stand it. As he listened to Sam Cooke or Otis Redding he thought about the ways that both men had died. Those early, violent, unexpected deaths made their music unbearably sad. Sometimes Ted felt, listening to the men sing, that they had foreseen their terrible fates. "James," Ted would yell, banging on the bedroom wall. "Turn it *down*, James."

There'd be a bump or a crash, and then the music would stop. "Sorry!" James yelled.

"It's cool, buddy."

And then James would start up with his compulsive string of questions. "Hey, Ted, you still like my hat, right, Ted? You still think my hat's cool, don't you? It's a cool hat still, right?" James's voice, muffled through the wall, was still so stricken with fear and urgency that Ted felt a chill.

"It's cool," Ted yelled. "Don't worry."

"Sally's coming for Christmas, right?"

There was usually a knock at the door a few minutes later. Whenever Ted opened the door James Dean almost fell into the apartment.

"I'm James Dean Garrett," he always said. "Movie star." James Dean liked to start every conversation by introducing himself with boundless excitement. Some mornings, when James's part-time caretaker had the day off, James would be dressed in his blue flannel pajamas with his denim jacket and tennis shoes, and his ever-present red plastic batter's helmet.

"I know it, James." Ted would say.

"Did you know I'm a movie star?"

"I know that."

"What do you think of this hat? Is this a cool hat?"

"It's okay," Ted would say.

"It's better than okay, isn't it?"

"It only matters what you think. If you like it."

James would shuffle his feet. "It's very cool," he'd say.

"Okay, then."

"It's cool, right?" He'd look up, all smiles. His brown eyes were wet, glassy, and they were frantic, always in search of something.

"You bet."

"I'm going to work now today."

"Can't wait for the weekend, right?"

"Yeah, that's right. Thank God it's Friday, right? TGIF." He'd wave theatrically and start running down the stairs, heading to work.

"You're in your pajamas, James," Ted would yell. "And it's Tuesday."

Since Ted was up, and there was no getting back to sleep, he'd change clothes and wait outside on the porch for James Dean to come back down. He'd watch the students on their way to class, hunched under the weight of backpacks, and he'd think how they were all trying to better themselves, and how their progress was as slow as that of other animals—of snails and tortoises—who carried weight on their backs.

Ted knew that James Dean would make his way to work alone, trudging along, listening to his Walkman. He had been doing it for years. But Ted also knew that James would have an easier time if he had company. Every so often there was a group of students who tailed James, and mocked him without seeming to mock him, asking if he was on his way to physics class, or if he had prepared anything interesting for organic chemistry lecture.

James Dean had a job in one of the campus cafeterias, wiping tables and carrying trays back to the kitchen, and keeping the creams and sugars and straws and plastic cutlery stocked on the condiment counter. He had a job in that cafeteria that included being the person at whom everyone stared with fear or pity or self-importance, a job that seemed to require him to walk around with half of his shirt untucked, his shoelaces trailing, plus the occasional indignity of an unzipped fly. There was always someone like James Dean Garrett cleaning up after college kids, working his way into their late night conversations and drunken imitations. There were those who laughed at him and those who defended him, those who stood him two-minute conversations every now and then, who clapped him heartily on the back as they strolled out of the cafeteria into the fresh air, the bloom of campus flowers and gossip. And there were those who left spectacular messes on their tables, unaware of his presence.

And so, on a series of cool fall mornings, Theodore Roosevelt and James Dean began their acquaintance. They rarely spoke as they walked. Any conversation they might have had would have been futile, for James Dean was only interested in two things: the popularity of his hat, and his status as a movie star. James and Ted had discussed these things so often that there was hardly need to speak. Ted walked slowly, with long, lanky strides, and James Dean fought to keep up with his stout plodding. They took a route to the cafeteria that passed through the center of campus. James Dean liked to see what was going on, because there was always something. Most mornings a religious fanatic was giving a sermon. He was the kind of fanatic who had given up all earthly concerns, such as cutting and brushing his hair, or wiping the fingerprints off the thick lenses of his glasses, or bothering to check the mirror to see if his shirt was on backward. "You're on a one-way bus ride to hell," he raved at passersby.

Each morning there was also a handful of student groups set up tables and handed out fliers. The college calendar was in perpetual bloom, with gay rights week, or election week, or Ronald Reagan appreciation week. Ted and James Dean were often forced to take fliers from the hands of eager students. The fliers were printed on bright-colored paper, and they advertised parties and concerts and meetings. Students dropped the fliers on the ground, and they blew around in the fall breeze, circling brilliantly through the air and skidding back down on the sidewalk. There were clusters of students playing guitar and reciting poetry. There was a sad midget who shuffled around the perimeter of the quad, playing an accordion. He dressed immaculately, in pressed slacks and short-sleeved white shirts, in suspenders and fedoras and polka-dot bow ties. He played the kind of lazy, dreamy music that introduced the scenes in films where American tourists lounged at sidewalk cafés in Venice, sipping wine under colorful umbrellas. On campus each morning there was also a gangly juggler. The juggler was always wearing the same black leather coat. It fit tightly down to the waist, where it tied with a belt, and then it flared out to the knee. The coat looked to Theodore Roosevelt like something that German soldiers had worn. The juggler's eyes were slightly different colors, one gray, one brown, and collectively, he was as strange and outstanding as a person walking around on stilts. He could juggle any four objects volunteered by the crowd, with weights and shapes as disparate as a textbook and a ballpoint pen. The juggler always kept a silver typewriter case at his feet, but he never opened to collect spare change. It was, Ted imagined, a matter of pride.

James Dean liked to stand at the back of the crowd and watch the juggler. "Hey, man," James called out on some mornings. "This is a cool hat, isn't it? This hat's cool, right?" The juggler was the only person who seemed not to hear James. He didn't seem to hear anyone. Ted felt, secretly, as though he and the juggler understood one another.

On one of these mornings, after Ted had walked James Dean to the cafeteria, he decided to drive over to his old house. It was something that had been on his mind for weeks, and each day he had resisted the urge to visit the house while his wife was at work. It had been two months since he left and he still had a key, and most of his belongings were still in the house. He and Annie had separated without fanfare. Ted had left quietly, with only a backpack full of clothes, a card table, and the books he couldn't bear to leave behind.

The house was immaculate. Annie had done away with most of Ted's favorite things—his bookcase made from lumber and stacked bricks, his framed portrait of Abraham Lincoln that had once dominated the living room, and his black manual typewriter with its delicate white keys that had sat for years on the dining room table. Ted rushed to the bedroom and opened the bottom drawer of the dresser. The four stacks of paper that comprised his dissertation were still there, mute, dull as a row of molars. Ted wasn't sure if he felt relief or anger at finding them there.

Ted searched for evidence of change in Annie's life. He noticed that the house had a sweet smell, and the light was different. Annie had filled the house with plants, and opened the blinds for them. Before, Ted had lived there in lifeless darkness, a habit he had carried over from college and graduate school. The plants seemed grotesque to Ted. Their vines with heart-shaped leaves crept over the edges of the pots and spread malignantly over the windowsills. The plants seemed as if they might move at any time, springing to dangerous life like Venus's-flytraps or like the angry apple tree in *The Wizard of Oz*.

The sweet smell of the plants was so overpowering that it sent Ted into one of his attacks. His eyes and mouth watered. He had a mad desire to rip the leaves off of the vines and eat them, to clutch fistfuls of soil, to throw the pots through the kitchen window. Instead he stalked from room to room, thinking of ways he could disturb things without being obvious. He poured half of a jar of spaghetti sauce down the kitchen sink and placed the jar back in the refrigerator, in exactly the position he had found it. He turned on the bathroom sink and turned it off so that there was a slow drip. He hid the remote control to the television under the middle cushion of the couch. He stole a white ankle sock from Annie's dresser drawer and put it in his pocket. She would go crazy looking for it. She had always scowled at the lost socks she found in Laundromats and parking lots, thinking their owners careless. Finally, Ted ran down the stairs and left the house, and sped away in his car like a bank thief. One of Ted's neighbors, Mr. Burnham, who was out trimming the hedges in his wading boots, raised the trimmers in a greeting that seemed equally friendly and threatening.

Ted noted that this was the first attack he had suffered in weeks. He considered, briefly, the possibility that leaving his wife and moving into the worst apartment he had ever seen in his life, that working nights and sleeping for only a few hours each day, that mopping floors and eating from cans—all of this seemed to be good for his health. It was something to enter into the file he was keeping on himself.

Mr. Roosevelt couldn't sleep, Ted wrote,
just thinking about the misery of his new surroundings, although it came as no surprise. Mr. Roosevelt had known for years that he would one day return to his rightful place as a person who lived in a strange brick building with a leaning chimney and cracked, curtainless windows, a building landscaped with lopsided shrubbery, with cement squirrels and ceramic geese spotting the lawn. This life had always been Mr. Roosevelt's calling. He had tried to do better. But nothing—no job, no amount of education— would change the fact that he had grown up alone in a small apartment, sitting in front of a television while his parents worked overtime at a shoe factory. His father still lived in that old apartment, complaining of heartburn and hernias on the few occasions a year that Mr. Roosevelt called to talk. The apple, Mr Roosevelt concludes, does not fall far from the tree.

Just eight weeks ago, Ted had needed a place to move into with his modest carload of possessions. He had been looking for the kind of apartment that he had lived in as child and as a college student. Something cheap, something with a steam radiator that operated with the turn of a knob, something he'd look back on wistfully once he'd made a mysterious fortune.

Ted wound up in a featureless brick building at the edge of campus. There was a handmade sign speared in the lawn that looked like it had been there for years. JAMESTOWN PROPERTIES, it read. APARTMENT FOR RENT. CALL MARK TWAIN. 329-9826. Ted remembered Jamestown Properties from when he was a student at the university. They had been renting student apartments for ages, and their buildings were the kind where second-floor bathtubs crashed magnificently through the ceilings of first-floor bathrooms. Ted knocked on the front door of the building. He started politely, but eventually resorted to banging his fist against the door. Finally a man answered.

"Are you really *Mark Twain?*" Ted asked.

"Don't start with me. Just don't even fucking start." Mark Twain sounded like a man who was holding in a lungful of smoke.

"My name is Theodore Roosevelt," Ted said.

"Fuck off, man," said Mark Twain, and he slammed the door.

Embarrassed, Ted waited ten minutes before knocking on the door again. Mark Twain answered immediately. He stood in the doorway scratching his stomach absently, looking at Ted with utter disdain. "I can tell you right now you don't want to move into this building," he said. Ted tried not to stare at the scar that ran down the right side of Mark Twain's face. It looked like a knife cut, something deep and purposeful that hadn't healed well. Mark Twain turned his back and started up the stairs. He motioned for Ted to follow.

It was the worst apartment Ted had ever seen. Paint was peeling from the walls of the three small rooms. The hardwood floors were stripped and splintery. The fixtures were stained and cracked, and the plumbing was bad. Even with the windows open, the air was stifling. Ted decided to take it.

During the brief tour of the apartment, Ted learned that Mark Twain had moved into the building many years ago as a young, blue-eyed go-getter, but now he was fat and balding, and sluggishly approaching middle age. He had been working on his dissertation for an unprecedented number of years. Broke, he had taken over the renting and maintenance of the building in exchange for reduced rent. Ted was told that he'd be sharing a bedroom wall with a forty-year-old misfit named James Dean Garrett, who would most likely be knocking on Ted's door for one reason or another every hour or so, and who liked to play his music as loud as it would go. No one had ever lived in that apartment, next to James Dean Garrett, for longer than three weeks. Ted could leave the rent underneath Mark Twain's door on the first of every month.

"My name really is Theodore Roosevelt," Ted told Mark as he was signing his deposit check. "My actual given name."

"Whatever you say," said Mark. He looked at Ted's signature, frowned, and handed him a key. It took Ted twenty minutes to move in.

That night, while Ted was deciding on the best placement of his card table and folding chairs, and debating the arrangement of books, there was a knock on the door. Before Ted even made it to the door, James Dean Garrett was introducing himself. "This is James Dean Garrett, the movie star," he yelled. His voice was husky and hoarse as a football coach's. He yelled all the time. It was his only way of speaking.

Ted opened the door. "Hey this is a cool hat, isn't this a cool hat?" James said, his speech fast and tripping. "This hat is cool, isn't it? It's cool, right?" He was wearing a red batter's helmet with white lettering. JAMES DEAN GARRETT, it read. MOVIE STAR.

"I heard someone talking about this hat," Ted said. "They were saying it was cool."

"It's a very cool hat. Very, very cool hat."

"It is. It's so cool that people are talking about it all over the place."

"You heard people talking about my hat?"

"I did."

"They liked it, didn't they? They said it was cool, right?"

"They loved it."

"They want a hat like this but they can't have one. It's cool, right?" James threw his arms up in a fantastic, Nixon-esque wave. "Bye," he said, and ran down the stairs.

Ted already knew James. He was a local celebrity, of sorts, famous with university students. As a graduate student, Ted had always thought of James as an adult child, someone who had mysteriously stopped growing with the passing of time, like a bonsai. His dark hair was shaved in a crew cut, and his skin was badly pocked. He still dressed like a teenager, in football jerseys and jeans and high-tops, and he still walked like a teenager, with giant awkward strides, with his head bent down and his hands jammed in his pockets. He was almost never without his baseball helmet.

James Dean had suffered an accident when he was fourteen. Ted had heard a variety of stories—that as a boy James had been hit in the head with a wild pitch, or that he had fallen down a flight of stairs, or that he had been struck by a car while riding his bicycle to school. The accident had left James with an odd mixture of characteristics. He had trouble taking care of himself, and he needed help handling the cooking and cleaning and laundry. He couldn't solve any kind of math problem, and he needed help handling his money. He was unabashedly friendly. He walked down the street, waving to people, stopping in at every store to say hello to merchants. He did uncustomary things. If he was out walking around the neighborhood, and he was suddenly thirsty or needed to use the bathroom, he'd knock on a stranger's door and ask to be accommodated. Most people in town knew him and stood him favors, thinking him harmless. But James was also capable, Ted sensed, of understanding what had happened to him—capable of the very adult notion of having been swindled. Ted saw this in James occasionally, in the way he sang those love songs with such anguish, in the compulsive repetition of his conversations, the rapid firing of his questions that had an edge of threat. James was also oddly insistent about his right to sit at local bars. It was a right that he treasured, and he went to bars nearly every night, simply because he was old enough.

James had a sister, Sally, who lived in Michigan. Sally visited once a year at Christmas, and James spoke constantly of her upcoming trip. "Sally's coming," he said, whenever it crossed his mind. The phrase was a comfort to him. It helped him mark the time, like the chime of a clock.

One day long ago someone had shown James Dean a picture of the movie star by the same name. James Dean in jeans and a white T-shirt and a leather jacket, leaning defiantly against a brick wall, squinting, a cigarette in his hand, half burned. James Dean Garrett had been so impressed with this picture, and so overwhelmed by the coincidence between his name and the movie star's, that he came to think of himself as a celebrity. And he became one. The only people who didn't know him were each season's entering students, who hadn't yet caught on, who stared in disbelief as James Dean sang out at the top of his lungs while he rode the university bus, rocking in his seat. "Let's get it on," he sang, along with Marvin Gaye, in his best falsetto. Anyone who didn't already know James was astonished by his first encounter with an entirely uninhibited soul.

Ted remembered that feeling, from his first year of graduate school. Now James was his neighbor.

Ted's boss was Leon, the big-bellied jumper-wearing supervisor, with his inch-long cigar and his habit of letting out long sighs and leaning back in unstable chairs. Leon whose desk drawer was stuffed with Twinkies and busted rubber bands and loose, mismatched keys, Leon whose third heart attack waited to spring at any moment, like a cheese-baited mousetrap. Ted liked Leon, who had hired him on the spot. One of Leon's night janitors had quit an hour before Ted walked into the office. The interview had been short. "Can you work nights?" Leon had said. "Can you push a mop? Can you take a joke? Can you clean up a floor-load of puke? Can you get up close and personal with a toilet?" Ted hadn't mentioned that he was a graduate of the university. Under the "education" section of the job application, Ted had only listed his illustrious career at Grover Cleveland High School.

Once a week, Leon gathered together his night crew to inform them of renovation plans and the schedule of pending university events, like parents' weekend and homecoming and the annual William and Henry James Convention. Ted liked the meetings, even though he sat alone and spoke to no one. Most of the janitorial staff had worked together for years and had formed the kind of friendship that Ted could never share in. It was hard for Ted to remember the names of his coworkers. They all wore the same pine-green jumpsuits, and they all wore expressions of disinterest that seemed to overpower any individual characteristics they might have had.

It was during one of these meetings that Ted first heard of the famed campus shoe snatcher. "Okay, folks," Leon said, sitting back in his chair. "Our guy has struck again." Leon liked to create a little suspense, like a police captain in a TV drama. He pulled a handkerchief out of his back pocket, blew his nose in two dry bursts, returned the handkerchief to its place. He opened his desk drawer and fished for a stick of gum, which he unwrapped slowly, and then chewed on for a minute and a half. "This time," he finally said, "things got a little weird."

Ted didn't know what Leon was talking about. But it soon became evident that a prowler was loose on campus, and that the university police were expecting the night crew to keep an eye out for suspicious characters. On his latest heist, Leon said, the shoe snatcher had hidden in the parking lot outside of one of the freshman dormitories, and waited until a girl had run out to her car to retrieve her backpack. As she leaned into her car, the snatcher had grabbed one of her ankles and pulled her down onto the pavement. He took both of her handmade moccasins. The girl also reported that the snatcher had started singing as he ran off. Something the girl couldn't quite catch. "How does it feel," she thought he sang, but the tune was so affected, so obviously sung in a false, tortured voice that she couldn't catch its meaning.

The meeting gave over to gossip, and the janitors placed bets. The shoe snatcher was, in their suspicious minds, a professor of philosophy, a white-collar townie, a drunken vagrant, or a third-shift university cop. "What's your bet?" asked one of the green-suited janitors. Ted wasn't sure who had addressed him. Though Ted was certain that the shoe-snatcher was someone ordinary, someone strangely familiar, someone like any of them, his answer was different.

"James Dean Garrett," he said, and the room filled with laughter.

These meetings were the only form of human contact that Ted had at work. Most nights he was utterly alone, working his way down long and empty corridors, left in complete silence. Memories returned to him at unpredictable moments, and he tried to catalog them in his file.

Today, Ted wrote,
while Mr. Roosevelt was supposed to be working in the Natural Sciences Building, he leaned dejectedly on the handle of his mop and browsed the glass display cases that lined the perimeter of the lobby. The cases were filled with specimens—the skeletons of armadillos, separated from their shells, diagrams of the verte-brae of dinosaurs, the teeth of great white sharks, fossilized im-pressions of the prints of extinct animals, amber stones gritty with the extenders of prehistoric insects. Most horrifying were the preserved animals floating in jars: a marmoset, a hammer-head shark, a naked mole rat. The fluid they floated in had turned pale green over the years, and it was nauseating to

Mr. Roosevelt. Perhaps the jars reminded Mr. Roosevelt of the
summer afternoon when the tap water was hot and clouded and
undrinkable, and his father had offered him a jar of pickle juice
to drink, and he had squirmed in disgust, and the father had
turned away sadly as though burdened suddenly with the
weight of all of his failures, and he retreated to his bedroom
with the jar and watched television behind a closed door, and
wouldn't let the young Mr. Roosevelt in for hours. To this day
Mr. Roosevelt is still saddened by the sight of a pickle. The color
also reminded Mr. Roosevelt of the notebooks with green paper
in which he attempted to write his doctoral dissertation. Mr.
Roosevelt had torn out and crumpled nearly every sheet in
thirty-seven notebooks, and balled paper was everywhere in
his apartment, like an infestation of failure.

That day Ted had seen Mark Twain on campus. Mark was
dressed for lecture. He wore a white dress shirt and tan slacks, both
wrinkled. Mark's tie looked as though it had been knotted years ago,
and that it had only been tightened and loosened on the occasions
that Mark dressed and undressed. He wore crew socks with dress
loafers. He was walking toward Ted, hurrying, his head down, a
stack of wayward papers tucked under his arm. Ted remembered
that feeling. Most likely Mark was unprepared for lecture, and he
was counting on the students' ability to discuss the assigned reading, which they wouldn't have read. It would be a long class. When
Ted thought about teaching, and the embarrassment of losing his
job at Baxter, which was the only chance he would ever have at
building a respectable career, he was surprised to feel relief.

Ted and Mark passed each other with only a nod of recognition.
Mark's hair was crazy and windblown, and it reminded Ted of a picture he had seen, of an aged, white-suited Mark Twain, who was
visiting the laboratory of the mysterious scientist, Nikola Tesla,
inventor of the AC current. In the picture Mark Twain was holding
a glass globe of the variety that fortune-tellers used. Inside the

globe were miniature bolts of lightning that Tesla had somehow managed to create. An electric current was running through Mark Twain's body, and his hair was standing on end. Ted was never sure if this was the effect of the electricity or fashion. A paragraph of Ted's dissertation had been devoted to this picture. He had been trying to create a link between modern art and modern science, for a reason he couldn't remember, and he thought that the picture explained everything.

What kept Theodore Roosevelt going through the semester, through the strange sensory attacks, and the loneliness and insomnia and bad diet—what kept him going was a bathroom.

There was a small bathroom in the Natural Sciences building, in the basement, at the end of a long, deserted hallway, that seemed to have escaped the notice of students and administrators and all other human beings on the face of the earth besides Ted and one other mysterious person who seemed to be using it as a personal library. The bathroom suffered from the effects of an overzealous radiator, a leaky ceiling, and weak water pressure. There was a mirror above the hand sink that was always fogged up, with all the heat from the radiator, and the moisture from a stream of water that slipped constantly down the wall behind the toilet. One of the most notable things about the bathroom was the floor. The floor's tiles must have been set decades ago, back when labor and craftsmanship were affordable. The tiles were miniscule, black and white, set in an intricate mosaic pattern of circles and triangles. Some were upturned, some cracked, and there were whole patches let loose along the fault line of a long crack that had swelled like a miniature mountain range. People didn't make floors like that anymore.

The bathroom's door was unmarked. No one had reason to suspect it was there. But someone had found it and taken it over as a salon. There were two twin mattresses, one on the floor and one leaning against the wall, that were arranged and covered with blankets to make a couch. A black-and-white picture of Charlie Chaplin hung on the wall. The picture had been torn from a book and secured to the wall with a thumbtack. It was a picture of the real Chaplin, without the pale skin and black-lined eyes and wild hair of the famous tramp. Here Chaplin was a tanned and trim and handsome man, with a slightly angled nose and a fine head of silver hair combed neatly in place. He was wearing an exquisite suit with a nice sheen, a silk tie, white loafers. He was standing in front of a black backdrop, leaning against a polished cane. He was the richest man in the world in that picture, or close to it. The longer Chaplin played the tramp, the richer he got, and this was, Ted had always imagined, the greatest torture of his life.

There had been a time in Ted's life when he was fascinated with people like this, when he thought that the progression of time was only a matter of losing valuables, that movies were worse since the onset of color and sound, and that modern stars were laughable imitations of the classic old-timers. Ted had been the kind of student who collected black-and-white photographs, who touched on the nostalgic sensibilities of professors by speaking out in class about his generation's lack of appreciation for geniuses like Voltaire and Groucho Marx. Ted had tried to discuss all of this and more in his dissertation, thinking himself a visionary. But when his graduate advisor had wept, truly wept, in one of their weekly meetings, Ted knew that he had gone hopelessly astray. He had cut his dissertation down to fifty pages, bowed out of the program with a Master's, and taken a position at Baxter. Annie had been devastated.

Next to the couch was a stack of cloth-bound library books whose paper was yellow and brittle with age. They were books Ted had never heard of, books that smelled of glue, books that cracked when opened, books with short columns of old dates stamped on their back covers. Ted was certain that he knew this person, this book-lender and interior decorator, whoever he was. This was someone who liked to study alone between classes, pursuing knowledge that he considered more important than his coursework. This person, Ted thought, was his unfortunate heir, doomed to write a dissertation that wandered pointlessly, intent on proving a connection between things as unrelated as motion pictures and the per capita income of Portugal.

Ted spent a few hours in the bathroom at the end of every shift, reading books that he had never heard of. Whoever had checked the books out from the library had a fascination with doomed characters living anguished lives. Ted read the novels of Nathanael West and Carson McCullers. They were novels about tortured loners who eventually wound up dead or deformed. After reading these books, Ted returned home in a strange mood, wanting nothing more than a few hours of dreamless sleep. But nearly every night was the same. He returned home at four or five in the morning and tried to sleep before James woke, played his music, and started asking Ted about his hat. But sometimes James even called out in his sleep, in a horrifying, boyish voice. Ted hated the sound of his own name when it was called out in need. It reminded him of his brother, Frankie, who had never once asked Ted for help. The last thing Ted wanted, while he tried and tried for sleep, was to think of Frankie.

Frankie had killed himself in high school, not long after their mother died in a car accident, and just after Ted left for college. Ted had never been sure if Frankie would have ended up any different if their mother hadn't died. As long as Ted could remember, Frankie was going off by himself. He walked to the corner pizza place each night after dark to play video games and drink root beer. He returned with a handful of scratch tickets curled in his pocket. Losers, all of them.

After school Frankie worked in a grocery store in the produce department, and he must have seen his future there. He was flunking all his classes and fighting with their father all the time, and perhaps Frankie saw himself, balding with bleeding gums, carrying a clipboard around the grocery store, checking in deliveries in a short-sleeve shirt and a clip-on tie, in polyester pants. There was nothing joyful in his life. He had been a piano player—their mother had taught him—but he never touched the piano after she died. Then they were both gone.

Ted hadn't thought that anything could be damaged by lack of use, that there was no better way of caring for something than letting it sit undisturbed, but the piano was in terrible shape. When Ted finished college, several of its keys wouldn't sound.

Ted's wife called one morning while he was watching a game show. "To the point," she said. "I need to know when you plan to pick up your belongings." She used the word belongings. She was clearly at work, in a meticulous mood.

"Ah, I don't know." Ted was keeping one eye on the game show. An old man was attempting to sink a five-yard putt in order to win a sports car.

"We can arrange something now," Annie said. "I have my appointment book here."

"Okay." The old man, who was wearing dungaree overalls, tapped at the golf ball so gingerly that it hardly moved. The audience erupted with despair.

"Do you prefer days? Because I'd already be out of your way. Ted?"

"Right. Days."

"Good," Annie said, and hung up.

Looking back, Ted had always felt this distance from his wife. He remembered an evening when he and Annie were watching the news, and they saw an interview with a fire chief who was grieving for the lost lives of six of his men in a warehouse fire. The chief was solemn, and spoke with his head bowed. He was in dress uniform, and there was a strange dignity in the gleam of its brass buttons and medals. One of the dead men, the chief said, had been found with his left hand in a fist. When they pried open his fingers, they found his wedding ring. He did that, knowing he was going to die, as a sort of farewell to his wife.

Ted had sat and thought about that, and also about his mother's sister, who had died in a fire at the age of twenty. She had been married just over a year and was eight months pregnant. Her husband had tried to drag her to safety by the hem of her nightgown. He had pulled so hard on the nightgown that it tore. When they found him, the torn scrap of flannel was still clenched in his hand, burned into his palm. They had both died. Ted's mother told that story only once. But she lived with it each day. She was so terrified of fire that she unplugged the toaster and the hairdryer and the coffeemaker after using them. Some nights she woke several times and fumbled in the dark to the kitchen, to check that the stove was off. She was also terrified, Ted thought, that given a similar situation in their own home, their father—passed out drunk on the couch—might not even try to save her.

Ted thought about these stories and wondered what kind of marriage he and Annie had. By that time Annie was in the kitchen, on a conference call with several of her bosses. She was a legal secretary, and she was so efficient and dependable that her bosses often included her in their late-night planning sessions. Annie was offering curt phrases of assurance at the same time that she was mopping the kitchen floor with furious strokes. Ted could smell the bleach she was using. Nothing escaped her. Not a single germ was allowed to multiply in a dark crevice. Not one hair loosened from her bun. They were a bad match.

Annie's phone call was the first Ted had gotten since moving. Earlier in the week, he had gotten his first mail. James Dean Garrett had left a Christmas card, though it was only mid-November. The card depicted the baby Jesus asleep in a manger, with an audience of adoring onlookers, man and beast. Inside, James's handwriting stretched across the card, wildly slanting and unruly, like a child's. HAPPY CHRISTMAS, TED, it read, JAMES DEAN GARRETT, MOVIE STAR.

Ted realized, looking at James's handwriting, that he was a person in James's life. James thought of him as a friend.

The night after Annie called, on the walk home from work, Ted noticed a rash of florescent pink sheets of paper stapled to campus telephone posts. They were handwritten warnings. GIRLS! it read.

WALK IN PAIRS AT NIGHT. THERE IS A SHOE SNATCHER ON THE LOOSE WHO WILL KNOCK YOU DOWN AND STEAL YOUR SHOES. DON'T BE A VICTIM. THIS IS NOT A JOKE.

Ted couldn't stop thinking about the sock he had stolen from his wife. All at once came the unbearable urge to gather up the signs, like a newspaper boy in reverse. He felt an urgent need for a wobbling bicycle and a canvas sack strapped across his chest, and the devoted following of a pack of neighborhood dogs. As he was tearing one of the signs from its post, Ted sensed a spooky figure standing close to him, and he saw a slight reflection in the corner of his vision. It was a blur of light and dark, like an oil slick. The figure moved away, and Ted saw clearly then the hunched back of the juggler, retreating in his long leather coat. He saw the boxy gleam of the juggler's silver typewriter case. Ted ran away, tearing down every sign he encountered and stuffing them inside his jacket and in each of his pockets until they were full, until he was fat with a false stomach and false hips, and he was sick from running.

Mark Twain spent his evenings on the front porch, working out fantastic equations on a legal pad, and venturing out on the front lawn occasionally to look at the sky. He also corrected student exams. Part of his work as a graduate student required him to teach a section of Astronomy 101. It drove him crazy. Whenever he had a batch of tests to correct he came knocking on Ted's door every hour, wanting an audience. "Listen to *this* asshole," he said once, standing outside Ted's door, shaking an exam. "'Galileo was crucified because he accused the Pope of thinking that the sun was a star.'"

"What an idiot," Ted said. "That Pope can just go fuck himself."
On the night of Ted's last sensory attack, he found Mark Twain

on the porch, smoking a cigarette, without a legal pad or an equa-tion in sight. "How's it going?" he said.

"You won't believe what happened."

"What."

"I gave an Astro exam to James Dean," Mark said. "Multiple choice. He passed." Mark's hair, what was left of it, was swaying in the breeze, out of control, like a silly Elvis fan.

"Good for him."

"He passed *and* he did better than half the class," said Mark. "I just hate these kids so bad."

"So do I." Ted thought briefly of asking Mark to come out for a drink, but Mark had been living life in the misery of that building for much longer than Ted had, and he was clearly past the point where a night of drinking would help. Ted left Mark alone to sit on the porch, absently fingering the scar on his cheek, comforting himself.

The bar that Ted chose that evening was an odd place. There was a country western theme—cowboy hats were tacked up on the walls, and a saddle was slung over the curved top of the juke-box. There were a few patrons who wore leather pants and spurred snakeskin boots. But the bar also ran videos of classic boxing matches on Saturday nights, which drew a mixed crowd of its own, from liberal English professors to factory workers to insomniac jan-itors. That night they were showing the fateful Ali-Liston fight. Ted remembered that Malcolm X had been at that fight, in seat number seven. This was just after he had been silenced by Elijah Muhammad for calling the shooting of Kennedy a case of chickens coming home to roost. At about the same time, Malcolm X came to realize that his murder was being plotted. He had been hiding out in Ali's training camp. It was an interesting fight. Fueled by a confl-ict between Muslims and Christians, favorites and underdogs. Ted had seen it a dozen times.

Ted did not notice when James Dean came in. He was waiting for the fight to start, and reading a book he'd borrowed from the bathroom. It was a strange book called *Hopscotch*. The book was about a bunch of artist characters who lived in Paris, who drank too much and got themselves into trouble, and who ran in a pack that seemed to be based on mutual disdain. Ted had never been to Paris, or anywhere else outside the country, and he went through alternating phases of admiring and mocking whatever part of the world whose coastline or literary talent was in fashion with the editors of good magazines that he subscribed to but never read. At the moment Ted was in an unkind mood toward the French, with their skimpy hats and crusty loaves of bread. Ted remembered that Theodore Roosevelt had been the first American President to visit outside the country while in office. There was a picture of T. R. on that trip, sitting atop one of the giant shovels that was being used to dig the Panama Canal. Ted's mind was crammed with these useless bits of information. He couldn't read a book or watch a fight without remembering a photograph or statistic, which he had inevitably tried to fit into his thousand-page dissertation. There would be no escaping these facts. They would never do him any good.

Ted was reading when he heard the distinctive opening strain of a bar fight. "Shut *up*, man," someone said, so loud that whole place quieted. Ted looked up and saw James Dean standing at the bar, wearing his jeans-and-leather-jacket James Dean outfit. Two men in white T-shirts were hunched over beers, their backs to James.

"Hey, I'm a movie star, you know," James said. "Didn't I tell you I'm a movie star?" He poked one of the men on the shoulder. The man whipped around and caught James by the wrist, and hit James in the face with his own hand. James slipped and fell. Ted heard his helmet crack against the floor, and he could tell even from where he sat that James was bleeding. Before Ted knew it he was standing right over James.

"Let's go, buddy," he said, and brought James up from the floor. "We're going home," he said. "It's going to be cool."

"I'm a movie star!" James cried out, his voice goosey. Blood was pouring from his nose. He pointed his finger at the man who hit him, who was making for the back door. "I'm *very cool!*" James yelled. Ted walked James to the front. James was crying, and his chest shook. "I'm James Dean and I'm a movie star!" he yelled, all the way to the door and all the way across campus. "Sally's coming at Christmas!"

"That's right," Ted kept saying.

When they were walking past the Natural Sciences building Ted decided to bring James down to the bathroom to get him cleaned up. James leaned against Ted as they walked down the wide set of wooden stairs to the basement. The stairs were so old, their creaking so eerie in the dark, that they were frightened of their own footsteps, as though they were the footsteps of burglars come to kill them in their beds.

James was mesmerized by the bathroom. When he saw it, he started coming back into character.

"Hey, Ted" he said. "*Look* at this place. Look at pictures. And the *bed* in the bathroom." His voice was stuffy and raspy, like a kid with a bad cold.

"It's pretty good, this place, right?" Ted pulled some paper towels from the dispenser and wet them down.

"Look at that *floor*. How many tiles is that, do you think?"

"I don't know."

"A lot, I bet."

"Yup." Ted touched James's nose with the paper towels and he flinched. "Here, you do it," Ted said, and backed away. He had never wiped a nose in his life.

James sat down on the bed and covered his face with his hands. Ted stood and looked at the walls. There was a new picture stuck up with a thumbtack. It was a black-and-white postcard of a very young W. C. Fields, back when he was a world-famous juggler, before he was a movie star. He was a thin man, then, with a full head of hair standing on end. His face was painted like a clown's. He was frowning dramatically looking down at his hands. Ted had heard from his father about Fields's juggling shows. The shows were such unique displays of skill and mock rage that Fields had become internationally famous. He had traveled the world, performing his wordless routine. In a way, once Fields went into film, his humor was limited to the English speaking world, and so he lost the majority of his audience.

Ted took the postcard down from the wall.

> *Dear Ephram,* it read:
>
> *Hi, bro. I found this in a bookstore and thought of you. I hope you're still at this address. The thought of writing and never reaching you is terrible. Please write.*
>
> *Love,*
>
> *Agnes*

Ted noticed that there was no address and no postmark. The card looked as though it had never been sent.

And then, standing there, Ted knew who it was. He wasn't surprised to find the juggler lurking in the back of his mind, though he had never suspected him before. Of course it was the juggler. It could be no one else. The juggler was a solo act, a loner who spoke to no one. He kept to himself. He was just the type to spend most of his day in the depths of a dark, unpopular building, in a bathroom at the end of an empty corridor, reading books that no one had checked out of the library in decades. He accepted letters but didn't write back. He was somebody's lost brother. Ted felt that he had known the juggler all his life.

When Ted looked over at James, he was asleep on the couch, breathing through his mouth. A wet paper towel was covering his eyes and nose. He was clutching the other paper towels to his chest. They were bloodstained, brilliant as a bouquet of roses.

Ted remembered a picture he had seen of James Dean and Ronald Reagan on the set of an ill-fated television program. Both men wore dark suits with brilliant white shirts, and their hair was slicked back. The scene they were acting out was set in an office.

James Dean was sitting casually in a chair, aiming a gun at Reagan. Ted had always loved that picture. No one would have thought, at the time, that James Dean would die so young, or that Reagan would become an American President.

Ted sat down on the floor, facing the bookcase, and picked through the new books. It was different, looking at the books and knowing whose they were. Ted leafed through a book about the islands of Micronesia, and the use of certain of those islands as testing sites for atomic weapons. There were U.S. Army bases on those islands that civilians were banned from. At night, some of the islands glowed with nuclear contamination.

Then Ted found a small volume of poetry titled *Bridge Suicides of the Nearsighted.* The book was made of rough paper, and its spine had been sewn by hand. The poems were about people jumping off bridges and leaving their eyeglasses behind, folded neatly on the ledge. Ted was sure that the juggler had written the poems. Everything the juggler treasured, it seemed, was connected with death.

Ted tried to remember what Frankie had done with his glasses. He tried to remember how it was that afternoon, when he had come home for Christmas break and found Frankie in the bathtub. He remembered how the room was still warm with steam, how the bath water was so red that he didn't see the knife Frankie had used until he was pulling him out. How pale Frankie was, and how thin. His face looked unfamiliar to Ted, because of the glasses. It was the first time in years that Ted had seen Frankie without glasses, and his face had changed in that time, in ways Ted hadn't noticed. Ted remembered thinking how his brother's eyes were more deep set than he had known, and how the bridge of his nose was sharper. And that they hadn't known each other, really.

Ted couldn't remember what had happened to the glasses, and this saddened him. He sat there wondering.

"Hey," James said. Ted didn't know how long James had been awake, or if he'd even slept at all. "Listen!" James yelled. He stood up and started bouncing on the balls of his feet. "Hey Ted, listen!"

Ted heard the sound of someone running, as fast as he could, down the stairs, and then away, down the opposite hall.

"Let's *go*," James said loudly. "This is *so weird*."

They ran up the stairs and out into the night, lit with the pinkish light of campus lanterns.

"Phew," said James. "Made it." He swept the back of his hand dramatically across his forehead. He had a sense of humor. "Hey, Ted," he said, having instantly forgotten his fear. "Sally's coming, right? This hat's cool, right?"

They started home. Ted chose a long, straight pathway that cut through the center of campus. The path was brightly lit by campus lights, and Ted could see nearly as well as he did in daylight. His vision was remarkably clear. He saw the girl coming from a hundred yards off. She was moving slowly, toward Ted and James, walking with a labored limp. She was carrying her backpack in her arms, held tightly to her chest. Ted could sense, even from a distance, that she was the shoe snatcher's latest victim, that she was making her way home, stunned and horrified, that her bare left foot was scuffed and bleeding from the walk, that she was a lonely freshman, startled by college life and the evangelists and accordion players and jugglers who gathered on campus to threaten students with the possibility of failure. Ted could tell that the girl lived by herself in a small dorm room decorated with pictures of her family, that she was crying like she hadn't cried in years, gasping through her mouth, that all she wanted in the world was the comfort of home, and that she would never again live without the fear of being seized.

Ted saw, at the same time, how truly strange he and James Dean would look in the eyes of this girl—James Dean with his batter's helmet and his bloodied nose, and Ted with the crazed expression of a person who hadn't slept in weeks. The girl had just collided with the desperation of the juggler, a lost person. Ted knew that he and James were part of the circus of adulthood that was so terrifying to this girl. The great triumph of Ted's senses was that he saw, even before it happened, that James Dean would ask this limping girl about his hat and about his sister Sally, and that the girl would flinch, that James would question her again and again, reaching out for the girl, speaking so fast that he didn't make sense, and that the girl would gather all that was left in common between people like her and people like Ted and James and she would flee, running as fast as she could away from the ruin that comes so inevitably with age, away from these great Americans.

The Hero of Loneliness

Seventeen years ago our town suffered an invasion of gypsy moths. The moths—who were not yet moths but still inch-long caterpillars, fat and black, with red spots and a coating of soft fur—made prisoners of the polite upper class, whose grand houses lined the edge of a forest of ancient oaks. Efforts were made to prevent the inevitable. Orange nets were draped over the branches of every tree. And so in the same way that circuses pitch their bright tents at the edges of respectable towns, threatening whole neighborhoods of decency and good taste, the moths marked their arrival. They thrived, crawled out of the forest and blanketed the streets. It was nearly impossible to drive. Soon the worms began to climb up the sides of houses. Women leaned from windows and poured pots of boiling water on the offending troops.

My mother went into labor when the infestation was at its exact worst. The way my brother Ephram tells it, my mother's safe arrival at the hospital, and therefore my safe delivery into the world, was nearly thwarted by the caterpillars, who were thick in the streets. Ephram says it was like driving on wet leaves, and that as he sat in the backseat of the car that morning he heard—even louder than the sound of my mother's heavy breathing—the sibilant squashing of caterpillars under the tires. By the time I arrived home all of the neighborhood trees had been scalped, every leaf savaged.

Seventeen years later, the worms plotted their return, and once again our town began its futile preparation. Canopies of orange nets were placed over the trees, and rumors started to circulate about a secret fleet of single-engine planes scheduled to fly low over our houses each night, leaving the neighborhood in a dreamy cloud of pesticide. As for Ephram, news of the returning gypsy moths prompted him to prepare for his escape from our town, an event that had been pending since his graduation from high school four years prior. Ephram purchased his first car, a refurbished 1972 Firebird with a brand-new silver paint job, and he vowed to leave upon sight of the first moth. Shortly after Ephram purchased the car he spotted the forerunner of doom wriggling on the front steps.

When Ephram announced his departure it was the end of the hottest summer in fifty years, and I was tired and nervous from a series of weekend trips in the backseat of my parents' car, staring out the window, bored as a grazing cow, touring a dozen of New England's college campuses, any of which might have harbored me as I became a younger version of my parents—a future lawyer and golfer, a future home shopper, a driver of expensive cars, a carrier of calfskin briefcases. The morning that Ephram told me he was leaving, headed to points south by way of Graceland, I wanted nothing more than escape.

"Take me," I said. I'd instantly calculated the pros and cons of the decision, like my father taught me. If I had to argue the point to him I would mention first and foremost the boredom of our privileged hometown, with its population of quaintly decaying historic homes and its constellation of white churches and automatic lawn sprinkler systems, and the dainty, deadening girlishness all of this was fostering in me. Secondly, there was the mystery of the South, which I had never visited but often imagined, with its tall glasses of lemonade and its front porch swings, with its rabid dogs hobbling

down unpaved streets and its bright red square dance barns. Need-
less to say there was Graceland, the lavish monument that a once
poor country boy had dedicated to himself. And finally, there was
Ephram, and the absolute certainty that he would never return.

Ephram simply turned away. He walked to his car, and stood next
to it for a moment. Then he did the unthinkable. He came back for
me. "Shift it in gear," he yelled from the front porch. "You got five
minutes to pack." I had been absolutely certain that Ephram would
leave me behind. I was a seventeen-year-old Catholic schoolgirl, a
knee-sock-wearing class president, a sullen book-reader, an overly
tall and horribly pale teenager with few friends, and a person who
had never once disobeyed her parents. In three minutes I heard the
Firebird's magnificent and impatient horn. I ran down the stairs
and out to the car without stopping to water the plants, to slide a
coaster beneath the water glass I had left on the dining room table,
to scratch the dog behind his ear, to write a note.

In only twenty minutes we were at the edge of town, and also at
the edge of the longest conversation we had had since I was twelve.
For the last few years Ephram had been a stranger, and riding next
to him was like riding with a character from a TV show that I had
watched many years back, before it went off the air.

"I'm surprised at you," said Ephram, and he punched me in the
arm. "My little fucking sister."

"How's it been going?" I said, and Ephram scoffed. I always managed to forget that he didn't partake in small talk.

"The weather, the Red Sox, everything's great," he said, in a deep
and formal and falsely optimistic voice, an exact imitation of our
father.

"Dad's gonna kill me," I said. "Dead."

"Agnes Mildred Clayson," Ephram said, looking at me over the
top of an imaginary pair of half-glasses. "You're a grave disappointment, young lady. I had *nothing* when I was your age. *Rats* used to
crawl under my bed at night."

We laughed. Ephram was speeding up the onramp to the interstate, and we were caught in the force of the steep curve that was turning us away from home. Our arms hung casually out the window, our fingers threading through the wind. This was living, I thought. This was what people did.

For the first few hours Ephram and I disclosed our particular objections to life in the Clayson household. It turned out that we had shared for the last five years, unbeknownst to one another, a mutual disdain for our parents. First we discussed our mother and her recent addiction to home shopping, calling toll-free numbers off the television screen at three in the morning, responding to the pleas of washed-up and bloated B actresses who have taken up the cause of starving third-world children.

"All those kids she's got taped to the refrigerator," I said. "It makes me sick! I mean, what am I, chopped liver?"

"I *can* make a difference," Ephram cried out, in a mockingly tearful voice. He raised his fist triumphantly. "I can get drunk every night and cry, and choke out the digits of my credit card number to telephone operators, and somewhere, somehow, a bowl of rice and a pair of shoes will be handed to a starving child!"

"And a glossy photograph will be taken," I added. "I can hang it on the fridge so every time I go for a candy bar I can think about what a great person I am." We snickered, snorted, scoffed. But when I looked at Ephram, who was staring blankly at the road, I wondered what he was really thinking about. I wondered how much he remembered of his former life as a toddler, living in project housing in Boston, almost starving to death, before he was adopted. It hadn't taken us long to reach the stony and sickening silence so characteristic of our family, so like the scraping of silverware against china at our dinner table, the morbid ticking of the grandfather clock.

I started in on our father, which I thought would put Ephram in a good mood. "Who am I?" I said, squinting, reaching out and swatting at the dashboard, groping like a blind man. "Is this the district attorney's office? Where am I? Is this Burger King?"

"Where am I going," asked Ephram. "Where have I been?" This

was our father, who refused to wear his glasses when he returned home from a day at the office. Our house was full of mirrors, and he couldn't stand the sight of himself. He refused to consult the rearview while driving, and had risked many an accident for the sake of avoiding his own reflection. Sometimes our father couldn't even stand to look at other people, and so he reveled in the fog of nearsightedness. He prowled the house in a haze, looking at his family without ever seeing the intricacies of our expressions, whether we were sad or curious or sarcastic. This way he could walk among his old possessions, stored in milk crates in the basement, without ever really seeing them, those old Beatles albums and Bob Dylan albums and Rolling Stones albums and Jimi Hendrix albums, his old guitar and harmonica, all the pictures of himself as a longhaired social worker, wearing corduroys and sandals and T-shirts.

Our father was the kind of rich man who had grown up poor and had never managed to forgive himself for amassing his fortune. His children were of particular concern. We were growing up rich and spoiled, and he snapped at us, exploding in fits of rage when we neglected to practice the piano or feed the dog or make good on a college scholarship. He was increasingly strange and he knew it. His beard was turning gray, and his tongue was brown from drinking coffee and smoking cigarettes. His teeth were edged in black. He barely opened his mouth to speak, as if there was something terrible running through him that might escape.

When Ephram and I exhausted the topic of our parents there was little left to discuss. We were into the trip's third hour, and the joy of flight was fading. There were long stretches of silence and sighing, and staring out the window at the cornfields and the desolate scarecrows that were nothing more than tattered clothes decaying on crosses.

In the middle of Pennsylvania, as we were driving through the mountains, Ephram pulled off for gas. The exit ramp was paved, but the road soon deteriorated to gravel, and it wound tightly down a woodsy hill. The road went on an on. It seemed that the car would lose control and we would slip off the road at any moment, crashing headlong into a thicket. "I don't like this," I said, but Ephram was paying his usual silent attention to the road, and he didn't answer. Finally we came to a crossroads, which was the center of a small town. There was a hand-painted wooden sign nailed to a telephone pole. WELCOME TRAVELERS TO OUR VILLAGE, it read.

"Oh, my God," I said "We're in a village."

There were three buildings positioned around the crossroads. One was a tall, three-story house with a giant porch that wrapped around all sides. The other was a shack, squat and windowless, that had been painted a brilliant pink. A giant sign was propped on the roof. "Look!" I said, pointing. "The Sugar Shack. Nude Girls!" Ephram ignored the shack and pulled up to the third building, a rambling general store that looked as though it had been built from the salvaged lumber of an ancient shipwreck. There was a single gas pump standing in the front parking lot of the store. Ephram pulled up and pumped gas, and then headed into the store to pay. I followed.

The store was something from a dream. One side was an old-fashioned ice-cream counter, with chrome detailing and red vinyl stools. The other half of the store sold, as a sign indicated, notions. There was a glass case of antiques, including jewelry and silverware and porcelain dolls. But the main feature of the shop was a collection of antique medical equipment. There were stethoscopes with colorful fabric cords, and miniature metal saws, and glass thermometers and peculiar, U-shaped clamps made of ivory. Strangest of all was a framed, poster-sized mosaic that depicted a doctor in the process of bloodletting a pygmy. The scene was set in a desert. The doctor was standing over the pygmy, holding a knife. There was a red gash in the pygmy's arm, and his blood was flowing into a large bowl. GOD BLESS MISSIONARIES was spelled out across the sky in white tiles.

I walked around the store, examining everything, but Ephram

was unmoved. He simply walked to the counter and paid the woman who was standing there, so still she at first looked like another curiosity, a wooden statue of a country woman in a plain yellow dress. The woman did not speak to Ephram when she rang him up, not even to announce his total. He held out the money and she tapped the counter with her finger, indicating that he should leave it there. She placed the change on the counter and stepped away from Ephram, looking away, shaking slightly, like a caught rabbit.

In the lot, Ephram's car was reflecting so much of the sun's glare that it was nearly invisible. We didn't notice that there was a stranger sitting in the back until we had settled into our seats. The stranger was bald, and he wore wire-framed glasses with small circular lenses. He wore a gray suit with a white shirt and a red tie. Nothing fit him quite right. The man's tie was looped in a messy amateur's knot, and the suit jacket was too narrow to button. Nevertheless the man gave off an air of frightening formality. He had a long and serious face, like the farmer from *American Gothic*. His hands were folded neatly in his lap.

"May I help you?" said Ephram.

"Just need a ride up the hill," said the man, as though Ephram were a chauffeur.

I was surprised when Ephram started up the hill without protest, without a moment's concern with the stranger. I leaned my head against Ephram's arm and glanced at the man through a veil of hair. The stranger sat perfectly still, staring straight ahead. He had impeccable posture. He kept a slight smile on his face, like he was holding in a secret.

Ephram stopped at the top of the hill to let the stranger out. As we started to drive off, the man called out. "You're a sinner," the man yelled to Ephram. "May God have mercy on your soul." The stranger held his hand out in a blessing and backed away, starting on foot up the ramp to the highway, due east, away from us. I watched Ephram's face in the rearview. His eyes seemed out of focus, occupied with some far-off thought or vision. He didn't speak for hours, and I busied myself with an inventory of roadside terrors: rusted mobile homes; clotheslines strung between trees, spotted with pink nightgowns and men's overalls and children's shorts pinned up to dry; tar-paper shacks and their accessory satellite dishes, their giant faces turned skyward, and cars without wheels or doors, and bicycles left on their sides in the yard; a preponderance of litter, fast food cups and paper bags; dead birds and opossums decaying under a haze of flies and the sickening circling of buzzards. All of these horrors dimmed with the setting of the sun, and soon there was nothing to behold but darkness, the oncoming headlights of eastbound traffic, a row of cars and their drivers headed toward an infinite variety of destinations. Ephram was enthralled by this, I could tell, by the possibilities of a life outside of his familiar circle. He looked dreamily at each exit sign, wondering what might be in store for him in towns named Sunnyville, Peytona, Salt Lick.

We spent the night at a rest stop. It was late August but the night was chilly and I woke shivering. I reached for Ephram, who was slumped away from me, his head resting against the window. He was cold. I sat up and looked at him. We had parked under a lamppost and the light was good. This was the first time since childhood I had really watched him up close. Ephram hated to be watched. He always spoke with his head down. Because he had two different colored eyes, one gray and one amber, and because he was shy about such a magnificent feature, Ephram hardly ever looked anyone in the eye. I saw for the first time that there was a defect in his right eye. The lid didn't entirely shut, and there was a gap where his eyeball was visible even as he slept. The eye roamed, and I flinched when I saw the iris roll across the gap. I thought for a moment that he could see me, and that he would wake when he sensed himself watched. But he was truly asleep. I reached over and touched his hair. It was so coarse that I knew he felt nothing.

Cars pulled up periodically. Couples emerged, hobbling toward the restrooms on stiff legs. The couples did not touch or speak to each other. They parted ways, using the restrooms and the telephones separately, buying snacks from the vending machines. They walked separately back to their cars, slamming the doors and digging in suitcases and looking out the windows. The travelers were tired of each other.

Ephram had only packed one parcel, and it glowed as it sat on the backseat. It was an old silver typewriter case, and its gleam was impossible to ignore. Inside the case was Ephram's mysterious book, which he had been working on since graduating high school. It was a long thesis on a staggering variety of topics, which collectively represented the sum of Ephram's self-directed education over the past years. My father was the only person who had read the book. He and Ephram had an arrangement: For every month that Ephram refused to enroll in college, he would have to research and report on a topic of my father's choosing. If any of the reports were unsatisfactory, Ephram would be forced to enroll in school. Each month my father spent an afternoon in his easy chair, pouring over Ephram's work, frowning, stroking his mustache. Eventually these reports became the only communication between Ephram and my father. Neither of them spoke about the other. I had only heard my father mention Ephram once in the past three years. "My son is an interesting man," I overheard him say once, after he had finished grading one of Ephram's reports. That was it.

I was crazy to read what Ephram had written. I reached into the backseat and placed my hand on the typewriter case, which was cold. Just then Ephram's half-closed eye rolled toward me, spookier than ever, and I couldn't betray him.

Insects buzzed against the overhead light, flapping their wings and knocking their heads against the glass, making terrible, futile sounds. By the time Ephram woke, many of the insects had succeeded in killing themselves.

Ephram is a heartbreak of a brother, a failure, a sulker, and a creep. He is obsolete. Strange as a telegram, a phonograph, an inkwell.

I have endured the sight of Ephram at countless menial jobs, first at the grocery—hunchbacked, slicing blocks of meat at the deli, a paper hat anchored to his Afro with bobby pins. I have watched him mop the floor behind countless counters, rowing the handle in sensuous circles. I have seen him standing on the street corner handing out circulars, shivering in his signature Army coat, his arm extended, the cheap yellow paper of the circulars flapping in the coldest of winds. I have seen him working at summer church bazaars, standing over a grill lined with sausage links, or perched on the high seat of the dunking booth, staring solemnly at the horizon, ignoring the line of teenaged pitchers hoping to sink him. I have seen him go under, dropped in the filthy vat of warm water, and I have seen him emerge, stoic as ever, to take his seat again. Of course there is his favorite job at the gas station, a career that allows him to read virtually uninterrupted for hours on end, a line of work that will likely support him in whichever strange town he decides to land.

This is my brother, the family's chagrin. He is the mess hidden in the garage—the wooden tennis racket, the rusted lawn chair, the mateless croquet mallet, the empty aquarium, the red plastic jug filled with spare gasoline.

I bear all of this knowing it is the life Ephram has chosen, one he prefers to the atmosphere of ivy league schools, with their monogrammed sweater vests and their upscale pubs and their green-shaded desk lamps. This is the life he designed, and it has failed him slowly. He has searched this whole time for an acceptable version of himself. As a boy he took to reading biographies, and many times he adopted the personality of whomever he studied. He took up juggling after reading about W. C. Fields, and he worked on his technique for years until he was able to handle bowling pins and knives and telephone books. When Ephram read about Muhammad Ali he studied Islam and he hung a punching bag from a rafter in the basement. When he read about Richard Pryor he developed a language of profane criticism so intricate and hilarious that it sparked, for one brief week, a trend in our otherwise humorless household that allowed us to point out each other's every goddamn motherfucking flaw.

A year ago Ephram stopped eating with the family. He let his hair grow into an outrageous Afro, six inches tall. He grew painfully thin, and did nothing but work at the gas station and watch old movies in his room, working his way through every black-and-white feature available at the video store. Recently he had stumbled on the films of Elvis Presley. Soon he began to commute to a small record store in Boston, the last place on earth where you could still buy an LP. Ephram paid good money for a stack of Elvis hits on 45s, and he listened to them for weeks. There was something about Elvis he couldn't let go of.

For the entire summer I was the last member of our family that Ephram spoke to. And even then it was subtle and silent, done in signals and glares. Ours was the language of umpires and third base coaches, of pitchers and catchers, the winks and nods and tugging of ears. "I'm black," Ephram said to me once, "but I've never *been* black." He said this as he was walking past the dinner table, where my parents and I were eating a silent meal. He walked on by. He was shirtless, and I saw the intricate bones of his spine. He was so thin, fragile as a fossil.

We drove without stopping, and crossed into Memphis the following morning. Ephram hadn't planned. He wasn't sure where Graceland was and we hadn't brought a map. In North Memphis, there were signposts without signs. We were lost, driving past a series of housing projects. Some of the buildings had been devastated by fire. There were windowless windows, and frames without doors. The bricks at the edges of windows and doors were stained with soot. People evidently still lived in these buildings. They sat on the steps and they roamed around the dirt courtyard, whose grass had been burned out by the worst heat wave in fifty years. The people moved slowly, suffering in the heat. Children played naked in the courtyard. They seemed ghostly, unsupervised, invisible to the adults around them.

"Don't these people have jobs?" I said. "It's a Tuesday afternoon. What are they all *doing* just standing around like that?"

Ephram didn't respond. He was having trouble driving. Broken stoplights hung from their posts, the lights burned out. At intersections, there were no rules of traffic. Ephram stopped, but hit the accelerator when he saw groups of men approaching the car in threes and fours, from all directions.

"What if we break *down*?" I kept saying. "This is crazy." I had never seen people like this, and I alternated between gawking and looking away. I knew that Ephram still recalled some of his impoverished childhood, before he had been adopted. He had spoken about it once, when we were teenagers, when we first began drifting apart. In the furthest recesses of his mind, Ephram had said, he remembered running down a long hallway of an apartment building, lit only by the red glow of the exit sign. He remembered crouching down to run his fingers against the grate of a heating vent. This was his earliest memory. The Claysons had adopted him when he was two. He had never really learned what his life had been like beforehand, except that it was so depraved that he had become a ward of the state.

"What if we break down? What if we keep circling around and around and we can't get out?" I said. I looked pleadingly at Ephram. He glanced at me, annoyed. "What would we *do*?"

"Shut up, you baby," he said.

"That's all you've said this whole trip!" Tears welled up in my eyes and streamed down my face but I resisted sobbing or gasping or even sniffling. Ephram had once complimented me on the way I cried. "If you have to do it," he had said, "at least you keep it to yourself."

"What should we do?" I said.

"What should we *do*?" Ephram mocked, using his best falsetto. "I'll show you what we'll do." He pulled the car to the side of the road and got out, and started walking toward a group of men who were standing in the parking lot of a boarded-up gas station.

"Ephram!" I yelled. "Come back!" But he continued walking. I rolled up the windows and locked the doors of the car. Ephram approached the men, who at first stood with their arms folded. But soon the men relaxed, joking and laughing. Ephram was animated, moving his arms and talking loudly. I had never seen him like that, and something startled me about the ease with which he had slipped into character. Eventually Ephram lead the men toward the car. They gathered around, all talking at once. "This is *classy*," one of the men exclaimed, and Ephram beamed. When the men walked off Ephram came around to the side of the car and pulled at the door handle, but it was locked.

"Open up," he yelled, "you baby." I waited until the men were a safe distance away before opening the door.

"Graceland," Ephram said brightly, after he settled in the car. "Two miles."

"Oh, thank God," I said. "Thank God, thank God."

"Have some faith," Ephram told me.

We parked, paid for tickets, and waited for the shuttle that would take us to Graceland. It was so hot that my clothes clung to me, and I kept wiping sweat from my forehead. Ephram seemed in a perfect state of comfort. He held his face up to the sun and basked. When the shuttle driver arrived and opened the door he was wearing a long-sleeved wool uniform. He also wore a black hat embellished with lengths of gold braid, and a leather glove on one hand. He smiled at Ephram and me, showing a gold front tooth and the flinty resilience of a person who had smiled professionally at tourists for several years.

"Welcome to Graceland," he said, speaking into a handheld microphone. "The most beautiful place on Earth." The driver had said this so many times that there was no longer any feeling left. It was a phrase so familiar and personal to him, like a phrase mumbled during sleep, that it was difficult for others to decipher.

All kinds of people were seated on the shuttle—middle-aged housewives in polyester pants and flip-flops, cameras strapped around their necks; black-clad teenagers, their hair oily and dark, their skin horrifically pale; men dressed like cowboys, the brims of their white hats soaked with sweat, their tight jeans tucked into snakeskin boots; rich New Yorkers with their expensive bags and manicures, and their high-heeled shoes and giant sunglasses. No one spoke. It was a short trip to the mansion and the driver barely had time to inform his passengers that the house had been owned by Elvis Presley and occupied by him, his friends, and his family during the greatest years of their lives.

I first saw the house through the shuttle window, as we were waiting for the crowd to file out. The house was much smaller than I had imagined. It was beautifully kept, with a glistening paint job and fine landscaping, but it looked no bigger than a regular home. I felt strange, suddenly, going into another person's house to look around. It was the first time that I had thought of Elvis, or any celebrity, as a person.

"You look just like Nat King Cole," a woman said to Ephram. "Did you know that?" I laughed. She was obviously crazy.

"No," Ephram said. "But thanks." He glared at the woman, who was short and fat, and who wore a T-shirt decorated with a cartoon sketch of a litter of poodles.

"I like your bag," said the woman.

"Thank you," he said, though his bag was an ordinary backpack.

"See my bag?" said the woman, holding it up. It was decorated all over with poodles. "I *love* poodles," said the woman. "Did you know poodles are prone to seizures?" she said.

"No!" he said, in feigned astonishment.

"Well, they are." The woman smiled. Her lips were painted tulip-pink. Just above her lip was a dark mole in the shape of Florida.

"Do you like poodles?" the woman said. But Ephram was tired of talking. He simply stared at her, fixing his strange eyes on her, and she backed away.

The tour guide was a cheery blonde girl with a thick southern drawl. She wore her hair in a high ponytail that was tied with a bow, and she managed to look like someone who had stepped straight out of the 'fifties. She began the tour with the story of Elvis's birth, explaining that Elvis had been a twin. Jesse Presley had been still-born. Elvis had lived. Surprised members of the tour clucked their tongues and turned to whisper to each other. Others nodded gravely, lowering their heads in respect, for they had known for the majority of their lives the first thing there was to know about Elvis, what they considered the initial victory and tragedy of his life.

The tour guide showed the group through several rooms, each with its own decorative theme. One room was filled with animal-skin furniture and rugs. There was a recording studio, an exercise room where Elvis performed martial arts in front of his admiring friends, and the kitchen, where Elvis's staff would cook whatever he wanted, whenever he wanted it, even if it was a six-week long, non-stop craving for meat loaf.

On the tour there was a man dressed like a cowboy. He was tall and thin, and he had a habit of perching one foot up on seats or rail-ings or benches, and lunging while he spoke. He stroked his long mustache and talked constantly throughout the tour of the famous people he had brushed shoulders with. He told how he had once seen Jerry Lewis in the Dallas Airport. In the days before the suc-cess of the PTL network, he had seen Tammy Faye Bakker sing at a revival. Most impressive of all, the man said, was his relation by marriage to Hank Williams's embalmer. "My cousin Jody got the call early that morning when Hank died," the man said. "'Jody,' they says to him, 'You'd better come on in to work. It's Hank Williams himself down here.'" The cowboy was speaking to no one in particular, but the whole lot of us, as if we were friends by virtue of a shared tour. "My cousin Jody said it didn't even look like Hank there at the morgue. Looked nothing like him. Jody had his work cut out, he said." The cowboy scanned his audience, looking for an attentive face. "Hank Williams was the best," the cowboy said to me. "But Elvis did all right, too, I guess."

The tour moved downstairs to the basement, which was the saddest part of the house. The walls were unfinished, made of concrete blocks. The blocks been detailed with a painted lightning bolt and Elvis's trademark letters, T.C.B., which, the tour guide explained, stood for "taking care of business." The tour filed through the basement to a small museum that housed some of Elvis's accumulated trophies—platinum records, awards, gold statuettes, and a variety of expensive costumes, including a magnificent white cape that was decorated with thousands of gold beads formed into a spread-winged eagle. It was in this museum that the tour guide first spoke of Elvis in the past tense. "It was prescription drugs," she said, "that killed Elvis. Prescription. He was in a great deal of pain," she said sadly, "and his doctors couldn't manage to help him."

The poodle lady began sobbing, clutching her bag to her chest, and the blonde tour guide bowed her head. The tour guide seemed to be accustomed to these outbursts. There were a million poodle ladies who flocked to Graceland, who had once been beehived teenagers screaming up at the stage, their arms outstretched, wanting, wanting to touch the cuff of Elvis's pants, to move their hips with him, to sway sensually in their poodle skirts. The poodle lady must have lived as a young woman with the torture of that terrible mole, and all of her fantasies about Elvis falling in love with a stout, ugly girl from the country were sometimes all that kept her going. She had been young once and she was crying about this more than anything, it was clear.

Suddenly everything was awful. I glimpsed my life with Ephram as a high school dropout, a vagrant southerner. I imagined our lives as residents of trailer parks—toasting hot dogs on sticks, watching our clothes spin despondently in the dryers of coin laundries, eating at all-night diners, choosing slices of glazed fruit pies from rotating glass cases and listening to the life stories of down-and-out truck drivers.

I once read an article in *Time* about a boy who was working the grill at a restaurant when lightning struck an antenna on the roof of the building. The shock had come through the stove and the spatula the boy was holding, and it ran up his arm and out his shoulder. He had explained in the interview how he still gave off a warmth from that arm that you could feel just by standing next him. There was some kind of current still running through him, the reporter confirmed, even months after the accident. This was the kind of experience I wanted, something thrilling and dangerous that would mark me forever without altogether changing my life. I wanted to go home. I didn't know how to tell this to Ephram, but it didn't matter.

Something different was happening to Ephram. He was at home here. He loved the heat, the ache of everything. He loved sleeping in the car, he loved the way train tracks crossed his path, watching the boxcars bang past, some with open doors. He loved the possibility of it, a ride in a direction you weren't even sure of.

I realized this during the last minutes of the Graceland tour. The poodle lady was sobbing violently, and everyone on the tour was hushed. We all looked at our feet and thought private thoughts, and I believe that at the very same moment Ephram and I knew we had reached our last hour together.

We walked sullenly to the shuttle, which dropped us off at the Graceland gift shop. I'm not sure when I lost track of Eprham. The cowboy had started a story about his great-great-uncle, who had married a girl who had known Billy the Kid in the biblical sense. I've always been enthralled by a good lie. Before I knew it I was standing at a counter in the gift shop, still listening to the cowboy and absently shaking a Graceland snow globe, and it was then I realized that Ephram was gone.

By that time Ephram was driving out of town, stuck behind an old wagon that he couldn't see around. The wagon was tall and boxy, trailing thick exhaust. The body of the wagon had been handmade out of wooden slats, and Ephram strained to see through the cracks. The worst smell he had ever known was coming from the wagon. Something was rotting in the heat, and Ephram felt a nauseated quiver in the back of his throat each time he took a breath. He tried to go around the wagon, but he couldn't pass. Then something flew from the truck, swirled in the air, and flattened against his windshield. It was a feather, a dirtied white feather, and Ephram knew then he was following a chicken truck, that these animals were on their way to slaughter, and that what he smelled in some part was their shit and their fear.

Ephram remembered a birthday party he had attended when he was young, at which his friend had been given a live chicken for a pet. The boy's parents owned a house on a two-acre lot, and they had already made presents of a sheep and three geese. Ephram had shown up to that birthday party wearing a dress. At the time, our mother was a feminist who encouraged everyone to question the conventional. When Ephram had admired a denim jumper in a storefront window, our mother had bought it for him. Every grown man, she thought, should count among his experiences at least one public appearance in drag. There was a picture from that party, a group of children in triangular paper party hats, sitting around a table, admiring a sheet cake. Ephram was the only black child. He was wearing the blue jumper over a white turtleneck, and he was looking away from the camera.

At the party, the chicken had walked unnoticed around the house, exploring, stopping here and there to peck at chair legs and balls of wrapping paper. By the end of the party the chicken had wandered off, and the guests had searched the house and grounds, finding nothing. The birthday boy had taken the chicken's disappearance in stride. He was the kind of rich kid who knew from an early age that most everything could be replaced.

Ephram couldn't pass the truck. He followed it for miles, waiting for the road to diverge. As soon as he got out from behind the truck, Ephram thought, he would let go of this memory from his former life, the absurdity of it, the strangeness of the people he had known. He would take whatever exit presented itself, and follow it without looking back.

How I know this about Ephram and his trip out of town is difficult to explain. I wasn't there in the car with him, really. It might just be too difficult to say out loud the truth of all of this, that I, Agnes Mildred Clayson, never really existed, that my mother and Ephram's mother, Mrs. Clayson, delivered a two-pound daughter the day that the gypsy moths were doing their worst, that I died within hours, that Ephram was allowed only the briefest glance of his sister struggling in an incubator, that he had pressed his hand against the plastic dome that separated us, and that after I was buried, and after a few years when nearly everyone had forgotten me, I was still growing in his mind, becoming his sister, his only friend in the world and only ally in a household so quiet that the only sounds at the dinner table were the ticking of the grandfather clock and the terse proclamations of Dan Rather. It is hard to say now that my whole life has been imagined by Ephram in the most intricate detail, that my brother has been the only person to know and love me, and that after all this time he is ready to let me go, that he is leaving home for good and starting a new life, and I am not coming along for the ride. Eprham will think of me less and less as he wanders the streets of Tuscaloosa or Galveston or Green Bay, carrying his silver typewriter case, juggling on street corners for spare change, sleeping on park benches and stables and in the basements of university buildings, touring the South by bus, trading yard work for home-cooked meals, taking the occasional job harvesting fruit or working behind the counter of small diners that ask no questions and pay cash at the end of the week. He will be the hero of loneliness. I wonder what will become of him, whether he will settle somewhere or wander forever. Whether he will eventually die among friends and family, or whether he will be found by a stranger, curled in a strange place, his head resting on his typewriter case.

Meanwhile I've been abandoned in the Graceland gift shop. This is where he left me. Soon Ephram will remember me as one remembers a character in a book or movie, and the remembrance will be vague, reduced to a slight rush of feeling, warmth or sorrow or nausea. In his mind I am simply a tall, pale girl standing at a counter examining souvenirs, perhaps shaking a snow globe, watching Graceland in miniature, watching the white flakes settle over that magnificent white house, and over the pink Cadillac parked out front, the snow falling so softly and peacefully. A nice dream, though we all know it never snows in Memphis. I stand fixed in his mind, twirling a rack of postcards, gazing at those beautiful black-and-white pictures of Elvis as a young man. The only images for sale in the gift shop are of Elvis while he was still young and newly rescued from poverty, still surprised to have his picture taken and to be dressed in such fine, tailored suits. What sells is the memory of someone young and promising, someone whose troubles haven't found him yet, someone who can't see the future for what it is.

The Tender of Unmarked Graves

Theodore Roosevelt's parents had named him after a President, hoping that their son would become a great man. Ted's greatness took its time, and when it came it was in a form that few people could recognize.

It was a chilly afternoon in late November, and Ted had strolled to work, kicking at fallen leaves. He had breathed in the scent of the season's first fires, of the smoke that was curling from the chimneys of the quaint houses that surrounded the university. It was a beautiful day. Ted descended the long stairway to the basement of the Natural Sciences building, and he unlocked his cart from its closet. Everything was in place, his broom standing upright in its corner, and for a brief moment Ted did not regret taking a custodial job, or leaving his wife, or living in a squalid apartment building with two crazy neighbors. He sensed, strange as it was, that he was just where he needed to be.

Ted began the day's work with his favorite bathroom. He usually saved the bathroom for last, but he saw from a distance that the bathroom's light was on, and he sensed that he would at last meet the strange juggler who had been living there. It had been a long time since Ted had seen any new signs of life in the bathroom. There had been no new books or photographs in recent weeks. And the juggler had stopped performing his usual morning show on the quad. Ted had walked James Dean to work nearly every morning, hoping to catch a glimpse of the juggler.

"Where's the juggler today, Ted?" James had started saying. "Doesn't he know I'm a movie star? He doesn't want to hang out with a movie star? He doesn't know what's up, anymore, that juggler guy."

Ted was unafraid as he entered the bathroom, and he was unafraid when he realized, at last, that he possessed the solemn greatness of a reaper, that he was doomed to witness some of life's most tragic moments. Ted had been the first to find his brother dead, lying in a bathtub full of blood. And now Ted was the first to find Ephram Clayson.

Imagine finding a dead man. That first moment, when you believe that he is sleeping on the floor. And then the slowly gathering realization that the peacefulness of his sleep is somehow strange. That the way his arm is tucked in toward his chest, and his hand curled gracefully over his heart, and his head tilted strangely, resting on a hard silver typewriter case—these things aren't lifelike. They seem staged, somehow, by an old-time Hollywood director.

Ted stood in the doorway of the bathroom for a long moment. The juggler did not move. Finally Ted approached the juggler and reached out to test his pulse. He placed two fingers on Ephram's neck, and it was so cold that Ted knew the juggler was long dead. Then Ted did something strange. He wanted to be good company. He knew his calling, and he didn't want a dead man to be left alone. He sat on the floor next to Ephram, and lifted his head and placed it in his lap. It had been a long time since Ted's brother had died. He had done the same thing then, resting Frankie's head in his lap, and this was the only moment in Ted's life that he hadn't come to regret. Ted placed his hand on Ephram's face, which was as pointed and fierce and bony as the face of a greyhound. Ephram's hair was smeared with dirt. The red clay of southern soil was all over him, smudged on his temple, on the sleeve of his jacket and the cuffs of his pants, on his fingers and under his nails. Ted sat for a long time, staring at Ephram, thinking about the strange and lonely life he must have been living.

When Ted had sat long enough, he lifted Ephram's head and rested it on the tile floor. It was then that he noticed a length of pink ribbon stringing out from the pocket of Ephram's long leather coat. Ted reached in the pocket and pulled out a satin ballet shoe. The toe had been worn through, and the arch was badly creased. But the shoe was still delicate, still beautiful. For reasons he didn't yet understand, Ted took the shoe and the typewriter case that the dead man had been using as a pillow and he carried these things to his custodial closet. He didn't want anyone else to have them.

Ted learned later that Ephram Clayson had killed himself with pills. At first no one at the university seemed to know the dead man. They had seen him juggling on street corners, that was all.

Eventually a professor of sociology came forward and said that he had spoken with the juggler once. The juggler had come to his office and tried to convince the professor to read a book he had written. But the professor was swamped with work, and he had asked the juggler to come back at the end of the semester. The professor said that there was something very strange about the juggler. He had shuffled his feet nervously, and he had mumbled almost incoherently. Now the professor was hoping that the manuscript had been found. He was curious.

Meanwhile Ted kept the manuscript in his apartment. It was a collage of nonsense and genius. Some was typewritten, and some done by hand in a strange, tiny print that slanted and looped wildly. The manuscript covered innumerable topics. The juggler had read extensively, and he had recorded his thoughts on each book. The manuscript wandered strangely, from Attila the Hun to the climate of Jupiter to the War of 1812. One chapter was devoted to an intricate genealogical tree, consisting of a variety of names and the various companies who had sent them mail. A web of lines connected the names and the companies who had solicited their patronage. The juggler thought he had deciphered scandalous connections between organizations. One woman had reportedly received mail from both the National Rifle Association and Greenpeace, and the juggler posited a conspiracy between environmentalists and conservatives.

Other chapters were personal. The juggler had taken meticulous notes on his sister, Agnes. He charted her development for years, making notes on her achievements in high school and her associations with various friends. In many ways the book was an autobiography, a catalog of the juggler's interests, both academic and personal.

Ted knew that he would never understand the book. Even still, he felt as though he was the book's rightful heir. He also knew, by virtue of the same instinct, that one day he would find his neighbor, James Dean, dead in his apartment, having suffered an accident or a heart attack. Ted knew that there would be others. This was his calling. A mad stork was hounding him, delivering the dead. Ted was becoming a rare breed of historian, a tender of unmarked graves, one who studied and remembered the lives of the least newsworthy Americans.

Ted carried on with his life, forgetting sometimes that a small corner of his apartment was occupied by the mysterious possessions of a dead man. Most days, the typewriter case and the ballet shoe sat unnoticed on a bookshelf. Only here and there, when the sunlight came through the window and reflected just right off the silver typewriter case, Ted would take the book from its shelf. It was a burden, reading the words of a dead man. Ted hated to imagine the live hand that had moved across every page, setting down every stroke of ink. It was spooky. Ted got the same feeling when he listened to the music of dead singers, when they let loose in the middle of certain songs, and their voices cracked. They were so alive, straining to express the depths of their sorrow.

Whenever Ted opened the typewriter case and leafed through the loose pages inside, he always read the last page first. The book's final passage was difficult to decipher, as it was written in the smallest of print. It seemed too private to read. But Ted could never resist. It was the last thing the juggler had ever written, and it seemed important. Ted thought that it was possible that he was the only person who remembered the juggler at all. And if he didn't read those last words, every now and then, the juggler might truly disappear from the earth.

Agnes, the last passage read:
You are growing distant, and I can't hold on to you for long. Even so, you are my only friend. I will always remember the day you were born. Have you liked this life? Are you lonely? You were born lonely. They wouldn't let me near you. By the time they let me touch you, you were already dead.